"Would [...] My Clothes Ended Up Like This?"

"They were filthy," Regan said with a testy edge to her voice.

"Now they're wet." Jake's voice was softer, more dangerous.

"I can see that," she said in a deliberately calm tone.

"Lady, if this is some kind of joke, I'm not laughing."

"I forgot, all right? I was tired. I fell asleep before I remembered to hang your things to dry. Everyone makes mistakes, even you."

He dropped the dripping clothes to the floor and moved toward her. "You have a good point," he said when he reached her. "But I've paid for my mistakes. Now it's your turn."

He braced one hand on the door a few inches from her cheek and leaned toward her.

One kiss, he told himself. And then he would be satisfied. One kiss and he could stop imagining what those soft angry lips would taste like. Just one kiss.

"No," she whispered. To him. To herself.

"Yes," he commanded. "Definitely, yes."

Dear Reader:

Sensuous, emotional, compelling... these are all words that describe Silhouette Desire. If this is your first Desire novel, let me extend an invitation for you to revel in the pleasure of a tantalizing, fulfilling love story. If you're a regular reader, you already know that you're in for a treat!

A Silhouette Desire can encompass many varying moods and tones. The story can be deeply moving and dramatic, or charming and lighthearted. But no matter what, each and every Silhouette Desire is a terrific romance written by and for today's woman.

April is a special month here at Silhouette Desire. First, there's *Warrior,* one of Elizabeth Lowell's books in the *Western Lovers* series. And don't miss *The Drifter* by Joyce Thies, April's *Man of the Month,* which is sure to delight you.

Paula Detmer Riggs makes her Silhouette Desire debut with *Rough Passage,* an exciting story of trust and love. Rounding out April are wonderful stories by Laura Leone, Donna Carlisle and Jessica Barkley. There's something for everyone, every mood, every taste.

So give in to Desire... you'll be glad you did.

All the best,

Lucia Macro
Senior Editor

PAULA DETMER RIGGS

ROUGH PASSAGE

SILHOUETTE *Desire*®

Published by Silhouette Books New York

America's Publisher of Contemporary Romance

SILHOUETTE BOOKS
300 East 42nd St., New York, N.Y. 10017

ROUGH PASSAGE

ISBN: 0-373-05633-8

First Silhouette Books printing April 1991

Books by Paula Detmer Riggs

Silhouette Intimate Moments

Beautiful Dreamer #183
Fantasy Man #226
Suspicious Minds #250
Desperate Measures #283
Full Circle #303
Tender Offer #314
A Lasting Promise #344
Forgotten Dream #364

Silhouette Desire

Rough Passage #633

PAULA DETMER RIGGS

discovers material for her writing in her varied life experiences. During her first five years of marriage to a naval officer, she lived in nineteen different locations on the West Coast, gaining familiarity with places as diverse as San Diego and Seattle. While working at a historical site in San Diego, she wrote, directed and narrated fashion shows, and became fascinated with the early history of California.

She writes romances because "I think we all need an escape from the high-tech pressures that face us every day, and I believe in happy endings. Isn't that why we keep trying, in spite of all the roadblocks and disappointments along the way?"

Prologue

"Jacob Hardin Cutter, having been found guilty of voluntary manslaughter, you are hereby sentenced to eight years' imprisonment."

Standing at rigid attention in front of the bench, Detective Sergeant Jake Cutter felt shock shudder through him like a nine-millimeter slug.

He had lost. The jury hadn't believed him.

Hard-bitten marshals, men who had once been his friends, surrounded him. Steel cuffed his wide wrists, shackles wrapped his ankles, a heavy chain connecting the two. His long confident stride restrained, he made himself walk erect, his head high, his eyes defiant, as he was led away.

The walls of Donovan State Penitentiary were towering, impenetrable, confining. The tall steel gate was electric, the sound it made when it closed behind him as final as death.

He tried to make his mind numb as his clothes were stripped from him along with his identity. The papers changing him from a free man to an inmate were stamped.

His possessions—a wallet, keys, his daughter's picture, his badge—were shoved into an envelope. The processing clerk handed him a uniform, bedding, a towel, a long list of rules and regulations.

A bored corrections officer in khaki led him through airless gray corridors, up slotted metal stairs, past tier after tier of concrete and metal cages.

Stunned, disbelieving, Cutter felt the hatred roll toward him. As though from a distance he heard the catcalls and cries of vicious angry men who welcomed any diversion.

"You're a dead man, cop."

"Too bad they ain't got no room for you in protective custody in one of them country-club prisons. You're gonna do some *hard* time, pig."

The guard stopped in front of a six-by-nine cell with blank concrete walls. No window. Bars that seemed a mile high.

"Here you go, buddy. Home sweet home for the next four years—if you're still alive to make parole."

The bars slid shut. Tumblers clicked and locked, to be unlocked only at the whim of others.

It was real, then. The humiliating arrest. The highly publicized trial. The verdict.

Cutter's big hands clenched the bars. Needles of panic drove deep into him. Sweat broke out on his forehead. Rage knotted his belly.

The law said he was guilty and had to be punished. He had lost his freedom, the job he loved, even his wife and daughter.

But no law, no jury of civilians, would ever convince Jake Cutter that he had done wrong. The court had taken everything but his personal code of right and wrong. Nothing, not even the daily horror of living like a caged animal, would take that from him.

He locked his jaw, struggling to keep the rage inside, fighting the terrible suffocating claustrophobia.

One second passed. Then another, suffered in silence. Another still, until a minute, an hour, an endless string of days, had gone by.

Cutter began to go cold inside.

He made himself numb.

He stopped caring about anything but survival.

The man he had been, the man who had cared too much, began to die.

One

The forest fire was out of control. On the steep slopes of the Laguna Mountains, seventy miles east of the sprawling San Diego metropolis, tinder-dry pines exploded into blazing torches, whipped into a frenzy by fierce winds from the desert.

In a few hours, maybe less, the fire would crest the ridge where prison volunteers with axes and shovels and chain saws were all that stood between the voracious flames and the small towns twenty miles below.

Swinging an ax at the far edge of the line, Jake Cutter no longer had a sense of time. He couldn't remember when he'd eaten last, when he'd been able to quench his choking thirst, when he'd slept for more than a few hours at a stretch.

It had to be close to midday of the third day. Or was it the fourth?

Thick acrid smoke had turned day into a hellish twilight that pressed down on a man like a stretch in isolation, wearing at him until he wanted to run and run and run. But

Cutter had no place to go—except back to his cell when he was no longer needed.

Over and over the blade bit deep, taxing even his powerful strength. The blisters on his hands had long since burst. Blood soaked into the leather of his gloves, making it difficult to keep a tight grip.

Under the fire-retardant coat, his shoulder muscles moved in a smooth powerful rhythm. His heavy forearms rippled, and cords of sinew stood out on his neck as he put his body into each blow.

As a boy he'd learned to swing an ax in these woods. As a man he'd spent countless off-duty hours backpacking on these slopes. But it had been a long time, almost four years, since he'd been free to hike anywhere.

He was a ruthless man now, thinking only of himself and his need to survive. In Cell Block D he was known as a man with ice in his veins and steel in his muscles, a man who had nothing more to lose. No one dared to cross Jake Cutter.

Suddenly, with a sharp crack, the tree he'd been chopping fell forward into the yawning canyon, crashing through the tangled underbrush. Impassively, the way he did everything now, Cutter watched it fall, then picked up his ax and moved to the next.

The roar of the flames was louder, the wind hotter. Suddenly, above his head, the small stiff leaves of an oak exploded into flame from wind-carried sparks. Seconds later, blackened bits of the parchment-brittle foliage began dropping on the weary men on the line.

"*Dios,* I got to rest, man."

Chacon, the prisoner next to Cutter, dropped his shovel and doubled over, breathing in harsh short gasps. Before Cutter could reach him, he'd sagged to his knees and crumpled over.

Cutter sent a quick glance toward the guard stationed a dozen yards behind the line, then knelt beside the writhing man. He bent low so that Chacon could hear him over the fire's roar.

"Take it easy, kid. It's just a cramp. We've all had 'em."

Chacon clutched Cutter's thick wrist, his face contorted in pain. "*Dios mio,* it hurts," he managed to groan. "A pain like knives." His skin was a sickly green under the soot.

"Try to relax, José. Take deep—"

"Hey, you men there! I ain't called no rest period. Get back to work."

Cutter mouthed a violent curse. Chacon's fingers bit into his wrist as a potbellied man with a thick neck and simian features lumbered toward them, a furious scowl on his face. His coat flapped open, revealing a large black revolver strapped to one beefy thigh. His massive hands lovingly cradled a twelve-gauge shotgun.

His name was Ivan Rhottman, and he was the corrections officer in charge of the furloughed prisoners. Cutter knew him as a bully whose sadistic cruelties to the men in his charge bordered on the psychopathic. The weak among the prison population feared him. The strong, like Cutter, hated him.

"What the hell is going on here?" Rhottman demanded when he reached the two men.

"*Por favor, señor.* A doctor," Chacon panted.

The others on the crew had stopped work to gather around, drawing an even more menacing scowl from the man with the gun.

"You men deaf or what?" the guard yelled over the roar of the fire. "I ordered you to get back to work."

Unwilling to risk Rhottman's wrath, the prisoners dispersed, returning quickly to their places. In the hellish world of prison a guard had total control—over a man's rigidly rationed privileges, his rare moments of relaxed supervision, his precious moments of emotional privacy. Days outside the walls, even days spent in heat and smoke and dust, were precious to men who lived in cages twelve hours a day.

Cutter squeezed the kid's shoulder, then straightened slowly, his narrowed gaze colliding with Rhottman's. In his days as watch commander in the western division of the San Diego Police Department, Cutter would have fired a man for subjecting prisoners to such emotional and physical abuse. Now he had to take the man's sadistic crap without fighting back. For another 314 days at least. Until his parole.

"You, too, hero," the guard ordered loudly, tobacco juice spraying Cutter's face. "Get your ass in gear, or I'll have you back inside before lock-down tonight. I ain't got no patience with slackers."

Cutter didn't move. Mere slits between dense blond eyelashes, his hazel eyes held a stillness that was more dangerous than the hottest fury.

"He needs a chopper, Mr. Rhottman," he shouted over the din.

"What for, a bellyache?" A vicious light flickered in the guard's putty-gray eyes.

"The rules say he's got a right to medical attention."

"I make the rules out here, Cutter," Rhottman spat out, "not you. You keep forgetting, you're no better than any prison scum, just like your fakin' buddy here."

"What if he's not faking?" Cutter's voice was as rigidly controlled as his temper.

A malevolent grin spread over Rhottman's face as he slowly let the barrel of the shotgun drop to Chacon's belly. "You fakin', José?"

"No, *señor*," the exhausted young man croaked. "On my mother's honor, I swear."

"Your mother ain't got no honor." Without warning Rhottman's massive arm drove the barrel deep into the cowering man's gut.

Chacon screamed, curling into a trembling ball like a terrified child. He retched, vomiting blood onto the dirt.

Cutter put his body between the kid and the guard. "That's enough, Rhottman," he bit out, his voice as deadly as the hard glittering light in his eyes. His big rough hands curled into bloody fists, but he kept them carefully at his sides. He would lose his parole if he struck a guard. That would mean another five years behind bars, plus a sixth tacked on for the assault.

A smirk of satisfaction crossed the guard's face. "Appears you got yourself an attitude, hero. Maybe you need a lesson in obedience. Starting now."

The barrel slammed into Cutter's belly, doubling him in two. Before he could stop himself, he came up swinging, his gloved fist smashing into Rhottman's viciously triumphant grin. The shotgun flew from the guard's hands, skidding across the hard dirt.

The guard let out a bellow, spit and blood flying from his battered mouth. "Kiss your parole goodbye, Cutter," he screamed, the veins on his neck distending. "You just bought yourself punitive time." His hand went to the thirty-eight on his hip.

Suddenly a noise like the crack of a high-powered rifle split the air above them. Both men looked up to see a burning branch hurtling toward them.

The world exploded in noise and flame. Men scattered. Rhottman screamed. Chacon covered his head with his arms. Cutter dove out of the way, rolling down the steep precipice into a tangle of chaparral.

The branch landed behind him with a violent crash, sending burning leaves and twigs cascading into the underbrush hugging the canyon rim. The tinder-dry brush exploded into flame.

Cutter was trapped. Below, the fire advanced with the speed of an onrushing tidal wave. Above, the rapidly igniting backfire was between him and the way out.

He wasted a few seconds orienting himself, then began running along the slope, parallel with the ridge. There was a deep gully surrounded by huge boulders a mile or so north. It was his only hope. If he was lucky, the fire might skim the top of the boulders without burning him to a crisp.

But his strength was nearly gone. He staggered, fell to one knee, pushed himself up again. Smoke stung his throat. The hot air seared his lungs. Tears ran down his cheeks, and he began to cough. Pain sliced his side, bending him nearly double. He couldn't breathe.

Suddenly, with the gully in sight, a hellish roar smashed against his eardrums. A fiery blast of wind ripped his hard hat from his head and tore at his face. He launched himself into the air, diving for cover. The earth came up to meet him.

Brilliant fireworks exploded in his brain, and he sank into unconsciousness.

Pain came first, throbbing with teeth-grinding intensity in his head. Then came the nausea, roiling in his stomach like hot lye.

Cutter tried not to move, tried to return to the icy blackness where the loneliness and bitterness and pain couldn't find him. But heartbeat by heartbeat, the inky void turned gray and then to hazy awareness.

He was sprawled on his stomach, one cheek pressed into the dirt, his arms outstretched, clinging to the earth.

God, he hurt. His head, his belly, his legs.

The silence was ominous, as though he were trapped in the eye of a hurricane. A soot-filled cloud hung low, directly overhead.

Slowly he pushed himself to a sitting position, then groaned hoarsely as dizziness swirled through him. His stomach cramped into a sharp knot. Nausea pushed at his throat. Blood oozed from a gash, hot and stinging, over his right eyebrow, blurring his vision.

Chacon's twisted face came to mind, bringing sadness and rage to join the pain. Had the others made it to safety in time? Or had that bastard Rhottman gotten them all killed?

Cutter's jaw tightened, sending clawing fingers of pain down his neck. Using the piled rocks as support, he slowly struggled to his feet and looked around. Smoke rose from the seared earth like steam. Blackened, half-burned trunks of once-majestic trees stood like ghostly tombstones in staggered rows. The air smelled musty, like dead ashes left too long in a grate. What had once been a place of peace and beauty was now a graveyard.

Figures, he thought with a cynical half smile. Nothing was forever. The more a man loved something, the more certain he was to lose it.

What now? he thought, slowly lowering himself to a nearby rock. So far the fire had burned in a wide arc, sweeping south to north, east to west, ahead of the hot Santa Ana winds, leaving the rugged western and southern slopes relatively untouched. One shift of the wind, however, and all that would change.

Cutter braced his hands against the rock below him and slowly shifted his gaze to the south. Smoke obliterated the horizon, but he knew what was beyond the miles and miles of trees.

Mexico. The border was less than fifty miles away. Four, five days' walk.

His heart began to pound. Excitement began to throb through his tired body like a powerful stimulant.

If the others were alive, they more than likely believed he had been killed when the slope where he'd fallen had gone up in flame. If the others were dead, the authorities were bound to think he'd died with them.

Why not let them go on thinking that?

His life was ruined, anyway. As a convicted felon, he could never be a cop again. The job was all he knew, all he had ever wanted to know. But one violent, rage-filled moment of listening to his heart instead of his head, and all that was gone.

Elaine had gotten her way, he thought bitterly. For the seven years they'd been together, she'd nagged him constantly to leave the force, to go to graduate school, to get a job where he wore a suit instead of a gun.

Their marriage had never been great, but he'd been a faithful husband and a good father. He had loved his wife as much as a blue-collar guy could love an uptown lady. His daughter was something else. She'd been a part of him, the best part, and he adored her.

Yeah, he'd probably spoiled her a little, too, he thought. Maybe that was why Elaine had gotten colder and colder over the years—that and the fact that he'd never made enough money to suit her.

Cutter swallowed the sick taste in his mouth. He hadn't heard from his daughter since he'd gone inside. More than three years of having his letters returned unopened, his phone calls refused, three years of missing her and wondering about her and aching to hear her small sweet voice calling for her daddy.

Cutter bowed his head. Every damn day since that first night inside he'd awakened with a rush of panic. Every night he'd prayed that sleep would take him quickly, so that he couldn't hear the hellish sounds of two thousand caged men.

Slowly his bloody hands formed into fists. No, he thought. He wasn't going back. Not to six more years of hell. He would take a bullet before he went behind those bars again.

Anything was better than prison. Better than spending a moment longer with a bitterness in his gut that ate at him until he wanted to smash his head against the bars. Better than swallowing his rage every time a guard with an attitude shoveled a load of abuse his way. Better than waiting for a shiv to slip into his back, no matter how careful he was.

If he remembered correctly, there was a small cabin on the eastern rim of Padre Canyon. Mountain courtesy demanded that it be kept stocked, just in case a lost hiker needed refuge.

A rare stiff smile crossed his hard face. Refuge was sure as hell what he needed right now. Along with a big cool drink of water and something to fill his growling belly.

If luck was with him, he would make the cabin by nightfall. A good night's sleep and some food, and he would be ready to leave at dawn.

Cutter got his bearings and then began to walk. In spite of his pain and exhaustion, he felt better than he'd felt in a long time. If he died on the mountain, he would take his last breath as a free man.

Two

"**O**h, no!"

A massive rock slide lay dead ahead, blocking the only road out. Regan Delaney slammed on the brakes and spun her vintage Triumph to the left. The right rear fender slammed into something immovable.

Regan flew sideways, smacking her ribs against the big wooden knob of the gearshift lever. The violent impact jarred her feet from the pedals, and the engine died.

"Dear God, where did that come from?" she muttered, trying to catch her breath. She blinked, trying to focus on the scene beyond the settling dust.

The smoke she'd watched from a distance now billowed from the canyon in front of her, turning the crevice into a giant chimney. Hot angry flames licked at the trees only yards from where she sat. Sizzling cinders and bits of ash rained onto the roadster's ragtop.

She was trapped. On her left a wall of granite rose skyward, higher than she could see. On her right was the fire. In front were tons of dirt and rock.

"Move, Regan. Get out of here now."

In a jumble of frantic movement, she managed to start the car and shove it into gear. Muttering a prayer to Saint Christopher, even though he was out of favor with the Church, she inched the car forward in a tight U-turn, praying the front wheel wouldn't slip over the edge. When there was room to maneuver, she tromped on the accelerator.

Wheels spinning, the TR-4 shot back the way she'd come, heading for the cabin she'd just left. Beneath the dusty hood, the thirty-year-old engine revved higher with each shift of the gears until it was dangerously close to the red line.

Gravel flew. The engine screamed. Somehow she managed to keep the car on the narrow twisting road.

Gradually the pounding in her ears lessened, and she eased up on the gas. She heard the sound then, a metallic clattering somewhere under the hood.

The car labored, slowed. The clattering grew louder. Beneath her damp T-shirt her heartbeat was fueled by an adrenaline rush, and her skin felt clammy, in spite of the August heat.

"Please, Rosie baby," Regan muttered. "Let me make it back before—"

Thunk.

The engine died. Immediately the car started coasting backward. Regan stepped on the brake and brought it to a gentle stop.

Having grown up with four older brothers who lived and breathed cars and a father who owned an automotive repair shop, she knew British sports cars better than most mechanics. She knew their idiosyncrasies, their foibles, the sounds they made. She knew what that awful metallic clattering meant. The engine had thrown a piston rod.

Hoping against hope, she twisted the key again and again. The starter ground, but nothing happened. The engine she had reconditioned part by part was frozen solid inside, and the cabin was still a good four miles straight up the winding road.

"I do not need this," she muttered as she jerked on the emergency brake, then leaned her forehead on the big wooden steering wheel and closed her eyes. The silence was terrifyingly loud.

"Well, this is another fine mess, Regan. A terrific way to spend your vacation."

She'd driven down to the mountains from the Bay Area for a rest. In the past two years, she'd miscarried twins, been told by her obstetrician that it would kill her to get pregnant again, been divorced by a man who wanted sons more than he wanted her, and was burned out on her job. This was the last straw. Absolutely, unequivocally, the utter end.

Regan began to laugh. It was better than crying. In fact, she never cried anymore. Not since the day she'd discovered that her husband's young, adorable, fertile mistress was three months pregnant.

Since the divorce, she had lived alone. No one was waiting for her to come home. No one was sitting anxiously by the phone to hear her voice.

Her family and coworkers at the Department of Child Welfare in San Francisco didn't expect her back for another week. Only Philip Sinclair, her neighbor and best friend, knew the exact location of the cabin he had lent her, and he had no way of reaching her.

The first thing she had to do, she told herself as she lifted her head and squared her shoulders, was decide what she was going to take with her back to the cabin. After that, when she wasn't so darn scared, she would decide what to do next.

One thing she knew for certain, though. She was on her own.

* * *

Four hours later Regan stood in the cabin's only door-way, too shocked to scream.

Someone had broken in while she'd been gone. The rear window was broken. Glass littered the floor.

The man who'd done it was sprawled diagonally across the only bed, apparently asleep. It was dusk, and the light inside was dim. Squinting intently at the face half-hidden in the pillow, she saw the rise of an angular cheek, the stubborn jut of a dirty stubbled jaw, a tumbled thatch of dusty-blond hair covering most of his forehead.

"Goldilocks and the Three Bears" came to mind, but she wasn't in any mood to be amused. In fact, she was furious. The cabin was private property, even though it stood on federal land. The man had no right to just walk in and take what he wanted.

Okay, you got that figured out, she thought. Now all you have to know is why he's here. Because he needs help, or because he's come to loot? Or worse?

Regan let out her breath in a slow stream and carefully lowered her heavy tote to the floor. On tiptoe, her sandals silent on the bare floor, she edged closer to the wood box by the fireplace. Without taking her terrified gaze from the man on the bed, she groped for a log.

"Hello. May I help you?" she asked loudly, her voice hollow, but trembling less than she expected.

The man didn't answer. He didn't even seem to know she was there. His eyes were closed. His massive chest rose and fell in a steady rhythm. She could hear the sound of his labored breathing.

He was a giant of a man, so big he dwarfed the double bed. His chest was almost as wide as the pillow, his torso lean, his legs long. Dressed in jeans and a cheap chambray shirt, rolled up above his elbows to reveal brawny forearms and thick muscular wrists, he lay with one arm outstretched, one knee flexed, as though he slept where he'd fallen.

"Sir?"

Silence.

Okay, what we need now, Regan, is Plan B. Find out what he wants. Uh-huh. Right.

Taking a firmer grip on the log, she tiptoed closer until she could see his face clearly. Her stomach dropped with a thud.

"Good Lord," she muttered on an indrawn breath. His cheek was bruised and scratched, his right eyebrow badly gashed and caked with dried blood. She couldn't tell his age. Early forties, she thought, and definitely a stranger.

Regan drew a shaky breath. What now? Plan C? She couldn't stand here all night with a log in her hand. Already her wrist was aching.

Maybe he was a hunter, she thought suddenly, trapped like her by the slide. Or a camper, trying to make his way down from the peak ten miles above.

Hastily she looked around for a rifle, a backpack, anything to give her a clue. When she saw the yellow fireman's coat lying in a heap by the bathroom door, she sagged against the wall by the bed and let her rigid shoulders go limp.

Big enough for two average-size men, the coat had US FOREST SERVICE stenciled in black across the back. The man was a professional. He would know what to do. But first she had to wake him up.

She returned the log to the box, then turned on the battery-powered lamp on the chest by the bed and stared intently at the face on the pillow. The texture of him was all male, a hard jaw, sharply planed cheeks, a straight nose hinting at arrogance, a slightly oversize mouth set in an unyielding line.

His hair, too many shades of blond to label accurately, was barbered, not styled. From the looks of the shaggy ends that curled rebelliously around his ears, he was long overdue for a cut.

Automatically she reached out a hand to shake him, then hesitated. Touching was as natural to Regan as breathing. An emotional person from the moment she'd let out her first bellow, she used hugs and kisses the way most people used words.

Whatever she felt, she expressed. Nothing was held back, not even the frequent bursts of temper that cleared the air and kept her from erecting walls against the people she cared about. But for some reason, she was reluctant to touch this man.

She told herself it was because he looked worn out and she didn't want to disturb him, but she had a feeling it had something to do with the intrude-at-your-own-risk set of that solid jaw and tight mouth.

She ran her hand down the side of her denim shorts, then touched his shoulder. His eyes flew open, then narrowed as he winced violently. Framed with spiky lashes darker than his hair, they were a deep hazel, glazed with sleep and dilated with pain.

"What the hell?" His voice was graveled and thick.

Before she could find her tongue, his arm shot out. A large bloody hand closed around her wrist. Pain raced up her arm, and she cried out.

"Answer me!" he snarled. "What the hell do you think you're doing?"

He jerked her closer, and she fell across the bed, her breasts squashed against his unyielding chest. In spite of his injuries, the man was terrifyingly strong.

Regan used her free hand to lever herself away from his too big, too masculine body. "Let me go, you idiot!" she shouted, trying to yank herself free of his hard fingers. "I was just trying to help you."

She jerked her chin at him, and long thick hair the color of caramel cascaded from the pins holding it away from her face.

Half-blinded by the pain hammering in his head, Cutter felt the shock twist in his gut. Sweet Lord, he'd nearly

slugged a woman before he'd come awake enough to realize he wasn't being attacked—a woman with flushed cheeks
and the wildest thatch of shiny brown hair he had ever seen.

So fast he wasn't aware he was doing it, he memorized her
features. Her face was almost triangular. Her chin was
stubborn, with a small but distinct indentation, a feminine
version of a cleft. Her eyes were almond-shaped and the
vivid clear green of spring grass after a rain. Her brow was
smooth, her nose impudent, her mouth a bit too generous
to be considered pretty. Her lower lip was caught between
her teeth, and her face was twisted with pain.

"Damnit, lady." Guilt put an edge on his hoarse voice.
"Don't *ever* come at a man like that when he's sleeping. I
nearly put a fist through your jaw."

He released her, then watched through slitted eyes as she
rubbed the reddening hand print on her wrist with slender
fingers.

"Is that how you treat everyone who tries to help you?"
Regan challenged angrily. Her face was hot and getting
hotter, the first warning sign that the famous Delaney temper was coming to a boil.

Cutter pushed himself to a sitting position. A hot twisting pain stabbed his belly, and he clamped his jaw tight,
fighting the nausea that rose in a suffocating wave. That
bastard Rhottman had busted his ribs, or damn near.

"Save your good deed for someone who wants it," he told
her when the pain eased. "I don't."

"Pardon me all to hell," she drawled. "The next time I
find a bloody unconscious man in my bed in the middle of
a forest fire, I'll be sure to leave him there to burn up."

Cutter called himself a few choice names for not making
sure the cabin was really deserted before he broke in, but he
had been hurting like hell by the time he reached the glade.
Exhaustion had taken the edge off his usual caution.

"Lady, after the day I've had, I don't give a damn what
you do, just as long as you do it someplace else."

Regan thought about the day *she'd* had. "Believe me, *mister*, I would love to be someplace else. Anyplace but here, in fact, but the only road out is blocked by about a ton of rock, and my car—which, by the way, I just spent two years restoring—blew up trying to get me back here."

He went deadly still, narrowing his eyes and then turning his head to look directly at her. "You're saying the only road down this side of the mountain is out of commission?"

Eyes that deeply hazel shouldn't be cold, she thought with a mental shudder. But his were. Cold and watchful, like the eyes of an outcast timber wolf she had seen once in a photograph.

She drew a breath, then said slowly and distinctly, "Yes, that's exactly what I mean. I hope you know another way down from here, because I sure as heck don't."

"Sonofabitch." The words seemed to explode from deep inside him.

Regan smiled without humor. "My sentiments exactly."

She stalked to the door and retrieved her tote bag. Rummaging impatiently through the clothes and other necessities she'd jammed into it, she finally came up with a rubber band.

Careful, Regan. You need this man, she lectured herself sternly as she bent from the waist and flipped her hair over her head. Using her fingers, she began combing the unruly tendrils into rough order.

Cutter ran his hand down his stubbled cheek, then scowled through the front window at the growing darkness. The light was almost gone. Only a fool would try to make his way over treacherous ground in the dark. At the moment, however, he was tempted to risk it.

"What are you doing here, anyway?" he challenged, ignoring the pounding in his head. "Didn't you hear the warning to get out?"

"Do you think I'd still be here if I had?" She shot him a disgusted look, then twisted the rubber band around her thick hair.

She straightened and threw back her head, her hair caught in a sleek ponytail that bounced against her neck. Her hair had a lustrous sheen, even in the dim light.

Cutter felt a ripple of awareness slide down his spine. It hit him then. For the first time in thirty-seven months he was alone with a woman. A woman with the kind of high-breasted figure that aroused a clawing hunger in a man and tested his resolve. He bit off a vicious curse. Why the hell couldn't she look like the female guards, hard as nails and about as appealing?

He swung his legs to the edge of the mattress, sucking in violently against the savage pain in his side.

Using the chest by the bed as support, he pushed himself to his feet. He locked his knees and stood rigid, head bowed, waiting for the dizziness to pass.

Standing a few feet away, Regan saw his jaw clench and cords ridge his strong neck. Sweat stood out in big drops on his forehead, and his skin was the color of wet ashes. Instinctively, she took a step forward, ready to catch him.

"Where are you going?" she asked with alarm.

"To check the fire."

"I'm warning you, do *not* pass out on me. I'm hopeless in an emergency." She was five foot nine in her bare feet, and strong, but this man was at least two hundred pounds of solid muscle and bone. Big as he was, there was no way she would ever get him back on that bed if he fainted.

Cutter raised his head and stared at a bright red-and-blue wall hanging directly in front of him, trying to keep it in focus. From the corner of his eye he saw her raise a hand toward him, then pull it back against her midriff. He noticed pink fingernails, some kind of red-and-white shirt hugging full ripe breasts, long legs that seemed to stretch forever, smooth and tanned and sleek.

His body reacted immediately, reminding him with a hard quick stab that he'd been without a woman for a long time. Slowly, gritting his teeth against the weakness that threatened to send him crashing to the floor with each step, he made his way to the door.

He leaned against the jamb for a moment, then walked stiffly to the porch rail and braced both hands on the rough wood. His thigh muscles felt shredded. His back felt as though he had been lashed with a whip.

Slowly he lifted his face to the breeze. It was warm and smoke-scented. He closed his eyes on a slow ragged breath. God help him, he was actually outside the walls he hated. Free to breathe air that wasn't stale. Free to listen to the rustle of leaves in the night instead of the nightmare moans of trapped men. Free to move more than nine short feet before he had to turn around again.

He opened his eyes, half believing he was back in prison and dreaming all this, the way he'd done for months and months. But this wasn't a dream.

Emotion clawed at his throat and burned his eyes. He was his own man again. Nothing was going to stop him. Not the fire. Not the vicious pain in his head and side. Not this woman.

Regan followed him out and stood a few feet away, arms crossed. Her relief at finding that she wasn't alone was rapidly disappearing. Whoever he was, and she realized suddenly that he hadn't told her his name, this big fire fighter was definitely bad company.

"What time is it?" he asked without looking at her. He seemed preoccupied with his own thoughts. Or was he always this unfriendly?

Regan held her arm to the light streaming through the doorway and looked at her watch. "Almost seven-thirty," she said, suddenly dreading the thought of night closing in. A fire could cover a lot of territory in ten hours.

"This your place?"

"No, it belongs to a friend. He rented it to me for two weeks. I'm a social worker in the Bay Area. For a while now I've been suffering from terminal burnout. I finally gave up trying to play Superwoman and drove down here for some

R and R. Little did I know I would end up in the middle of a forest fire.''

She moved to his side and looked up at him. Sweat shone on his face, and he was breathing heavily. Suddenly she was ashamed of herself. The man was hurting badly. No wonder he wasn't in the mood to be polite. She decided to forgive him.

''I'm Regan Delaney,'' she said in a let's-start-over tone.

From the corner of his eye, Cutter saw her lips curve expectantly. She was waiting for him to introduce himself.

Lie, he told himself. You need the practice. But lying had always come hard for him, even in the line of duty. Besides, what good would it do? He was too big, too easily identified. Four years ago, his picture had been on the evening news for weeks. Jake Cutter, the rogue cop, the guy who had to do hard time because the system had a hole in it.

''Name's Cutter.'' In the eyes of the law he was a cold-blooded killer. If she recognized him, he was in trouble. The last thing he needed was a hysterical woman on his hands.

''Is that what people call you?''

''Mostly. First name's Jake.''

Regan rolled the name around in her mind. It was hard-edged, masculine, with a no-nonsense ring to it. She had a theory that a person's name influenced his character. His certainly had.

''I'm glad you're here, Jake. I thought I was going to have to walk down the mountain by myself. I could have done it, of course, only I'm not all that great with directions. Give me left or right, and I'm fine. North and south, east and west, tend to confuse me. Philip, the man who owns this cabin, says that's because I'm almost completely right-brained.''

His jaw moved as though he'd clenched his teeth, but he said nothing. Obviously a man of few words, this guy Cutter.

Following his example, she stared out into the purpling twilight. Soon the silence began to make her edgy. She liked noise around her—voices, music, laughter. Getting along with this man was going to be heavy sledding if he was always this quiet.

"When I first saw the smoke, I thought it was just another grass fire," she said drawing a startled sidelong glance from those unusual eyes. For some reason she had a strong feeling he'd forgotten she was there. "With the drought and all, there've been dozens already," she added when she saw she'd gotten his attention.

"A twenty-five-thousand-acre grass fire? You've got to be kidding!"

Her brows swooped into a frown. "I know people, not fires," she said crossly, jerking her chin at him. "That's your department. Speaking of which, I certainly expect the forest service to pay for the window you broke."

Cutter saw temper blaze in her eyes and decided she was trouble, the kind he sure as hell did not need right now. Somehow he had to figure a way out of this mess before he got himself caught and sent back to finish his sentence.

"Lady, unless the wind shifts, in two days there won't even be a cabin here, let alone a few pieces of broken glass."

For the second time since she'd met this man, Regan was shocked into silence. He's right, she thought in dawning horror as she slowly let her gaze trail over the deceptively peaceful clearing.

Twilight was normally the noisiest time in the small glen, the hour when the birds returned to their nests. Now, however, the sky was conspicuously empty and silent. In the space of an afternoon, the air that had been crystal clear was hazy with smoke.

"Two days? Are you sure?"

Cutter ignored her question. Just being next to her was getting under his skin in ways that even prison hadn't gotten to him. Forget it, Cutter. You're outa here as soon as you find a way to get her elegant little butt to safety.

"Exactly where was that rock slide?" He seemed to remember an old logging road about seven miles down that intersected the main road. If it wasn't too overgrown, she might be able to use it to circumvent the slide. Provided he could tell her how to find it.

Regan told him, then went on to describe her near miss and the frantic trip back up the mountain. With each word, she noticed that he seemed to grow more and more remote.

"How do you know your car is out of commission?" he asked when she finished. "Maybe you flooded it?"

"I've owned British sports cars since I was sixteen. I've restored three of them from the engine up. I know what it sounds like when a rod is thrown."

"What direction was the fire traveling?"

"Uh, west, I think. Toward town."

Cutter's sore hands tightened around the railing until he could feel blood wet his palms again. "You sure you haven't seen anyone in these parts? A ranger, maybe, someone checking the area?"

Regan shook her head. "You're the first living soul I've seen in eight days. What about you? How did you get here?"

"I walked."

"Walked? From where, for God's sake?"

"Heartbreak Ridge. I was cutting a firebreak, and the fire crested. I got . . . separated from the others."

"Where's Heartbreak Ridge?"

"North."

Regan nodded slowly, although she had only the vaguest idea of the area. She'd tucked the map she'd gotten at the ranger station into her tote. When she had a chance, she would get it out and study it. Just in case, she told herself.

"But they'll be looking for you? Your crew, I mean?"

"No one flies over a fire after dark. The air currents are too tricky."

Regan saw the cynical twist to his mouth and wondered what she had said wrong.

"So . . . there's nothing we can do until morning?"

"You might try praying—if you believe in a God who listens."

The tone of his voice told her that he didn't. She didn't have to hear the steel in that slightly husky baritone to know he was a man who didn't think he needed anyone, even a higher power. A man who made his own rules, followed his own path.

All of a sudden, the meadow seemed even more silent, more threatening. She shivered, trying to ignore the nagging feeling that she and Jake Cutter might die together on this mountain.

She wanted to like him. She *needed* to like him, so that she could trust him with her life.

Putting strangers at ease, getting them to trust her enough to confide their troubles, was part of her job. She rarely had a problem, maybe because she was naturally empathetic and dedicated to helping. She liked people. They liked her.

Not this man, however. It was as though he resented every kindness she tried to show him, disliked every gesture of friendship she made toward him.

She refused to give up. The thought of spending what might possibly be her last moments on earth with a stranger, a man she didn't even like, made her sick to her stomach.

She made her voice conciliatory. "I'm sorry I startled you, but I was afraid you wouldn't wake up."

"I'm sure as hell awake now," he muttered, his mouth jerking upward at one corner. Probably in disgust, she decided, although, in another man, that surprisingly sexy quirk would almost certainly indicate wry humor. But his mouth had a controlled hardness to it, as though he had forgotten how to smile.

She told herself she should be wary of this man. That he had the marks of violence on him and the look of a loner stamped on his face. Not that she was afraid of him, she assured herself, but funny things began happening in her stomach.

"Are you hungry? I can fix you some soup."

"I'd rather have whiskey."

"Sorry, I don't drink. I have mineral water, though."

Cutter thought of Elaine and her Junior League friends who drank designer water by the gallon. Not because they liked it, but because it was trendy. He scowled.

"Got any cigarettes?"

"No, I don't smoke."

His sigh was heavy. "Figures."

"How about a hot bath. This place might be lacking in a lot of the things you're used to, but it has a propane water heater and indoor plumbing."

She flashed him one of her patented smiles, the one her brother Sean teased was more deadly than one-hundred-proof Irish whiskey. A strange look crossed his face, a look she was suddenly glad she couldn't read.

"Lady, you can't begin to imagine what I'm used to." His voice was so cold, so utterly bitter, that it sent shivers up her spine.

He turned quickly, then staggered. At the same time Regan moved to help him. They collided, her breasts smashing against his hard chest. His granite-solid thighs slammed against hers, and she reeled.

One huge arm came down to crush her shoulder. The other came up to wrap around her. Her knees buckled under his weight, but somehow she managed to keep them both upright.

"I told you not to pass out on me."

Cutter couldn't seem to focus. Everything was moving around in strange, disjointed patterns. He took a deep breath. Then another. The small anxious face close to his became two, shifting slowly into a white blur surrounded by a soft brown halo.

His eyes closed, and his head fell forward drunkenly. His forehead touched her shoulder as his arms found her waist and held on.

Unexpected emotion escaped his iron control. It felt so damn good to hold a woman against him. To feel her move, to smell her perfume. He'd been numb for so long. So many endless days, so many suffocating black nights, alone. So damn alone.

Regan felt his arms tighten until she thought her ribs would crack. "Jake, you're hurting me," she managed to gasp. "I can't breathe."

From somewhere deep inside he found the strength to lift his head. He couldn't let himself want this woman. He took a deep breath, then another, trying to clear his mind.

"I'm okay now," he muttered, squaring his shoulders and lifting his chin.

His slurred voice told her otherwise. He was obviously at the end of his strength, no matter what he thought. She wrapped her arms around his wide torso and urged him toward the door.

"Let's get you back inside before you take us both down."

Somehow she managed to support him until they reached the bed. By the time he was sprawled on his back again, they were both breathing hard.

Regan saw his strong throat working and realized he must be terribly thirsty. "I'll get you some water," she said with a hint of apology. She started toward the kitchen area, then turned back to ask, "Does your head hurt?"

His irritable grunt told her more than any words.

"Hold on," she ordered, patting his shoulder. He stiffened, but she pretended not to notice. "I have some aspirin in my bag."

Cutter watched her rummage through her tote again, hauling out clothing, paperback books, a large orange bag of chocolate candy.

"I know I have aspirin somewhere. I always— Aha! Here it is!" She held up a small bottle, gave him a quick smile, then walked away from him. Her hips moved with a subtle sex appeal that sent his pulse rocketing.

The tightness in his belly coiled into a hard, painful knot, and the need tormenting him increased until it was a hot ache. I don't need this, he thought angrily. Not now.

Cutter eased onto his side and stared at the wooden paneling across the room. For months, in the restless hours before he had learned to exhaust his body during the day in order to sleep at night, he had longed for a woman's softness next to him.

But with the same force of will that had kept him alive, he'd made himself stop dreaming about a woman's hands on his body. Stopped wanting the soft things a woman brought to a man's life, the private, intimate things that gentled the savage in him. He would stop himself again.

The throbbing in his temple took on an edge, like steel striking steel, like the clang of his cell door when it shut behind him. The ache in his head became a sizzling white noise. And then he slid into blackness.

Three

It was quiet, too quiet.

Wide awake the moment he opened his eyes, Cutter held his breath against the instinctive panic that always came when he first awoke and saw the bars.

Instead, to his shock, he saw pine walls, colorful furniture and a woman with dark hair asleep in a chair by the bed.

Sonofabitch, he hadn't been dreaming. He bolted upright, then sucked in his breath against the hot stab of pain in his side. A quick glance at the window told him it was close to dawn.

The gray haze seemed thicker. The fire was still burning. Maybe cutting off his escape. Damn it to hell, he hadn't meant to sleep.

Cutter mouthed a silent curse, then slid his hands down his whisker-rough cheeks. He caught a flash of white. A heavy layer of gauze had been wrapped around both palms, covering the worst of the raw places.

I'll be damned, he thought as he gingerly touched the piece of tape covering half his forehead. The lady had patched him up after he'd passed out. Stripped him nearly to the buff, too, he realized with a scowl, and cleaned off the worst of the dirt.

He flicked a gaze to the long fingers lying relaxed and open against her satin-smooth thighs. From someplace in his imagination he conjured up an image of those hands running over him when he was most defenseless. Wiping the blood from his face. Cooling his hot skin. Easing off his dirty, sweat-stained clothes.

Knowing he shouldn't, he let his gaze rest on her huddled body. She was so close that he could smell the clean powdery scent of her skin. If he reached out his hand, he could run his fingers through the shiny brown hair spilling over her shoulders. In the light from the lamp it seemed almost golden and very soft, the kind of soft a man liked to wrap around him when he made love.

At the thought of burying his face in that enticing silk at the moment of release, his body stirred in a way that even his steely control couldn't prevent. He felt a moment of bitter anger. At himself, mostly, for getting himself trapped here with a woman who reminded him of all the things prison had taken from him.

Narrowing his gaze against the hammering in his head, he stared at the face half-hidden by the heavy fall of glossy hair, at the gentle curve of a flushed feminine cheek, the smudge of tiredness under the feathery lashes, the twin lines of worry between swooping brown eyebrows. She looked worn out, yet she had let him sleep in her bed.

He closed his eyes, feeling a terrible tiredness tug at him. His survival instinct was strong. Even before he'd become a cop, he'd had a sixth sense about people.

There were two kinds of men—those he could trust to walk through a door with him, those he couldn't. There were two kinds of women, too—those a man married, those he didn't.

Regan was definitely a woman who deserved the protection of a man's name, a woman to be cherished, a woman to grow old with. Once, a long time ago, he would have enjoyed matching wits with her. Another time, another place, and he would have waged a hard battle to get her into his bed.

No matter how many times he told himself it would be a mistake, he wanted her. Without words. Without promises that would have proved meaningless, anyway. Without gentleness.

Yeah, he had choices all right, he thought grimly as he opened his eyes and took a deep slow breath. He was a free man. Free to walk away from her right now. Free to hate himself for the rest of his life if he did.

He threw off the covers and swung his legs to the side. At the sudden movement, bright lights exploded before his eyes. His head began to swim, and he felt as though he was going to be violently ill.

He slitted his eyes and held his breath, waiting for his head to stop swimming. Damn, he wanted a cigarette.

Where the hell were his clothes? he thought irritably, shooting a head-splitting look around the small room. He saw his boots standing side by side near the chest. Her tote bag and an open first-aid kit were on the table next to a bowl and a cup. His coat was hanging on the back of a chair. He couldn't see the rest of his clothes.

He closed his eyes and fought the urge to put his fist through the nearest hard object.

"Wake up, Regan. I need my clothes." His voice was hoarse, and his throat felt as though he'd been chewing sandpaper. He tried to swallow. It hurt too much.

"Mmm?"

He gripped her shoulder and shook her hard. "Regan. Wake up."

Her long lashes fluttered upward. She sighed, then narrowed her gaze against the light from the lamp. "What's wrong?'' she mumbled. Her voice was sleep-slurred and husky.

You're what's wrong, Cutter thought wearily. I can't leave you here, and I sure as hell don't want to take you with me. "I need my clothes."

"Clothes?" Regan blinked, trying to focus. Slowly the blur in front of her sharpened until she saw a muscular male chest dusted with golden hair. A lean torso splotched by a wicked-looking bruise the size of her hand. Wrinkled drab-olive shorts. Long sinewy thighs.

Her gaze jerked upward to a stubbled chin, a hard cynical mouth, a pair of watchful bronze eyes that seemed to take in every inch of her in a blink.

"How do you feel?"

"Like hell." His voice had rusty edges, as though it hurt to speak. The bandage on his head was splotched with fresh blood. The heavy stubble on his jaw was more pronounced after a night's growth, adding the weight of years to a face she decided had never really looked young.

She managed a drowsy, one-sided smile. "I feel like I just closed my eyes," she mumbled. "I warn you, I don't function well on two minutes of sleep."

Cutter tried not to notice the sleek length of suntanned skin beneath the hem of her shorts. Before he could stop it, desire dug deeper into his tired body.

The ache in his body put a sarcastic bite in his voice. "Feel free to go back to sleep once you tell me where you put my clothes."

Regan frowned. Her brain was fuzzy. "In the bathroom, I think."

She sat up and pushed the sleep-tangled hair away from her face. Her cheek was flushed where it had pressed against her arm, and her eyes had a little-girl innocence in the hazy morning light.

Cutter felt something hard and hurting pass through him. He ignored it, just as he ignored most things that had nothing to do with survival.

Sucking in against the stiff muscles in his side, he reached for his boots. His thick wool socks had been shoved into the left one.

Regan yawned, fighting to keep from slipping back into the cozy warmth of sleep. Hot prickles shot down one arm, the one that had served as a pillow.

"What time is it?" she asked.

"Be dawn soon."

"Oh my God, the fire!"

In a scramble of arms and legs, she uncurled from the chair and ran to the front door. Opening it wide, she hurried to the edge of the porch. The smell of smoke stung her nostrils and irritated her throat. Above her head, the gray cloud seemed thicker.

"Definitely closer," she muttered, whirling so fast her bare feet skidded on the dew-damp boards. Her hip banged into the side of the house, and she muttered several unladylike words as she limped into the cabin.

Cutter was standing in the middle of the room, staring down at a sodden, dripping bundle of clothing. As soon as she entered, his head swiveled toward her.

"Would you care to explain how my clothes ended up like this?" His voice had the steel-on-steel ring of a man holding himself under tight control.

Regan fought down a pang of guilt. After she'd started the generator, she'd put his bloodstained clothes in the tub to soak while she fixed herself a bowl of soup. After she'd eaten, she'd been so tired it had been all she could do to curl up in the chair and close her eyes. She had forgotten all about his wet things.

She closed the door and leaned against it, one hand still on the knob. When faced with a man as big and as angry as this one, she figured the best defense, the *only* defense, was a strong offense.

"They were filthy," she said with a testy edge to her voice.

"Now they're wet." His voice was softer, more dangerous.

"I can see that," she said in a deliberately calm tone. "You're getting water all over the floor." She glanced pointedly at the puddle spreading around his big feet.

"Lady, if this is some kind of a joke, I'm not laughing."

Prison had taught him patience, but this woman seemed determined to test it.

Regan had a feeling her defense wasn't working, but she had never learned how to back down once she'd plunged into something with her usual lack of caution.

"I forgot, all right? It happens. I was tired. I sat down to rest. I fell asleep before I remembered I meant to hang your things over the porch railing to dry. You don't have to get nasty about it."

Their eyes clashed. Cutter noticed that her hair was in a sexy tangle about her face, and temper was smoldering in her eyes. Wildfire, he thought. That's what she is.

"Lady, this is not nasty. This is indignant. I think I have the right to be annoyed, don't you?" He dropped the dripping clothes to the floor and moved toward her.

"No, I don't. Everyone makes mistakes, even you."

He thought about the mistake he'd made that had sent him to prison. He thought about the long empty nights as alone as a man could be. He thought about the excitement in his gut when he considered making love to this woman.

"You have a good point," he said when he reached her. "But I've paid for my mistakes. Now it's your turn."

He braced one hand on the door a few inches from her cheek and leaned toward her. His furred chest hovered over her breasts. His muscular bare thighs were only inches from hers. His body wasn't touching hers, but Regan found herself wondering what it would feel like if he took her in his arms.

"Seems we have a problem here, Regan," he said in a voice that vibrated through her like a powerful rush of emotion. "What do you think we should do about it?"

"Jake, be serious," she said on a sharp intake of breath. "I came in to tell you the fire's closer. I saw the flames in the canyon last night when it was dark. I think we should leave don't you?"

"See any flames this morning?"

"Well, no..."

Regan felt invisible shivers of excitement move over he skin. She absorbed them, fascinated by the sensation. She had grown up flirting with her older brothers' friends sharpening her feminine wiles until she'd had them al wrapped around her slender, perfectly manicured finger. Bu her usually reliable sixth sense warned her that a nice safe flirtation with this man wasn't possible. Nothing about he feelings for him were safe.

"Did you see any planes? Helicopters?"

He nudged the cascade of curls from her shoulder witl the back of his hand. Her hair was as soft as he'd though it would be. Like a vixen's belly.

"No, no planes or...anything." At the brush of his hand against her neck, Regan felt her breath catch.

He pushed his hand deeper into the gold-tipped thick ness. Soft curls slid against his wrist, sending a shuddering jolt of need to his groin.

"Then stop worrying."

"But—"

"You want me to walk down the mountain in my skivvies?" The corner of his mouth lifted, not much, bu enough to draw her gaze. Why had she thought his moutl was hard? It wasn't hard now. She felt herself being drawn to test that rare softening.

"Shouldn't we be packing or something?" Could he hea the shiver in her voice? Would he think it was the dawn chil that put it there?

"Relax. We have time."

Cutter let his gaze brush her mouth. Her lips were beau tifully formed, with just enough fullness to make a mar wonder how they would feel against his.

One kiss, he told himself. And then he would be satisfied. One kiss and he could stop imagining what those soft angry lips tasted like. Just one kiss.

His hand curled around her neck and pulled her toward him. His head bent.

Her hands flew to the solid wedge of muscle padding his shoulders, intending to push him away. He didn't move. Regan felt the strength in those unyielding muscles and realized she was helpless against this man.

"No," she whispered. To him. To herself.

Everything about him—the tension knotting his brow, the slow burn in his eyes, the aggressive tilt of his head—warned her to retreat. Power had only been a word—until she'd met Jake Cutter. Now she knew what it meant.

"Yes," he commanded. "Definitely yes."

He fitted his mouth over hers, calling on all of his hard-won restraint to limit the contact to a quick taste. But when her mouth clung to his with sweet fire, his control exploded into a hunger he couldn't fight.

He took a step forward until she was pinned against the door. Her breasts cushioned him, her warmth easing the ache in his gut. She was all that he'd thought she would be. Warm, sweet, pliant.

He framed her face with his hands. She didn't resist. Her eyes drifted closed, and he saw anticipation and something that looked like surrender settle over her face.

Even as his mouth took hers again, he told himself it was to prove a point. That he was free to kiss her. Free to leave. Free to do any damn thing he wanted.

His mouth took hers over and over. Her lips were moist from his need. Her breath heated his. Her arms clung.

His dreams had never been like this. Nothing in his experience had been like this. He felt consumed, enveloped, absorbed. The black images in his head faded in the sunshine that was Regan. The brutal memories haunting him disappeared in the thunder of his heartbeat.

His arms dragged her away from the door and more tightly against his chest. He felt the pressure of her breast and was tempted to explore their soft shape with his hands. But the need in him was for her mouth, for the sweetness he tasted there, like sustenance for a man too long hungry. He was drunk, drunk on her, on freedom.

Her hands roved his back, his spine, his buttocks, urging him closer. He had expected fire. He hadn't expected an eagerness to match his own.

His body hardened. Hunger clawed him and he heard a groan, then realized it had come from him. With an effort of will, he dragged his mouth from hers and buried his face in the fragrance of her hair.

Regan's hand stole to his neck, soothing him, trying to release the tension knotted there. It's all right, she wanted to say. I understand. And she did.

Something was driving him, something that rode him with barbed spurs, something he needed to bury in the hot explosion of passion. She'd felt the same crushing ache herself, when she'd heard that Tony's new wife had given him the son she couldn't.

She'd hurt then, known that there was something lacking in her. Something elemental and innately feminine.

She made a small involuntary sound.

He lifted his head and looked at her. A frown tugged at the bandage above his hairline and fanned lines into his temples. "Did I hurt you?"

"No. It's just that I...I've been divorced for over a year. It's been a long time since I've been kissed."

She'd gone wild inside, but he didn't need to know that. In spite of her impetuous nature, which had gotten her into enough hot water to clean half the city, she had always been extremely cautious when it came to sex.

She'd had one lover, her husband. And she'd held him off until he'd put an engagement ring on her finger. Not because she was being manipulative, but because she believed in love and commitment first.

It was the fire that had made her act so recklessly, she knew. In some basic way, the fact that she had to trust this man with her life had created a bond between them. The kiss was merely cementing that bond, she assured herself.

She rested her head on his shoulder. Nothing would happen that she didn't want to happen.

So she was divorced, Cutter thought. What kind of a fool would let this woman go? he wondered. If she'd been his...

But that would never happen. His arms were still around her, and he knew he should let her go. Somehow he couldn't find the strength. It felt so good holding her, inhaling the clean scent of her hair, listening to her soft breathing. He felt himself begin to heal in places that had been raw for a long time.

Too soon, he felt her stir. One kiss wasn't enough, he thought. Not nearly enough. Reluctantly he looked down, preparing himself to let her go.

Her pupils were wide and turbulent, her expression soft and vulnerable. Hold me, he wanted to beg. Make me whole again. Make me feel human.

But a man didn't say those things. Not a man like Jake Cutter, who had always been the strong one, the one who fought battles for people who couldn't, the one who kept his own pain locked up tight, where no one could see it and think him weak.

"I'm sorry about your clothes," she said with a small smile.

He brushed a wisp of hair from her cheek. His hand wasn't as steady as he wanted it to be. "A man could go crazy around you, trying to figure out what you're going to do next."

Was he making promises? she wondered, and then knew that he wasn't. She wouldn't let herself be disappointed. She'd had promises from Tony, believed them, until they'd proved to be empty.

"Philip has some clothes here. Maybe they'd fit you."

"Is he six foot five?"

"No. But he's big."

"Big?"

"He was a linebacker at Berkeley years ago. Most of his bulk has shifted. Too many cherry truffles."

Cutter saw a sparkle in her eyes and realized she was teasing. It was such a small thing, commonplace in her world and so completely alien from the life he'd led for so long. No one teased in prison. Taunted, hurled vile insults, made lewd suggestions, yes, but no one teased.

He felt himself begin to smile, something else he'd rarely done in the past three years. In fact, he wasn't sure he'd ever smiled in prison. She had no idea what a precious gift she was giving him, but he did.

"What do you mean, shifted?" It was hard to get the words past the lump of unexpected emotion in his throat.

"Mostly to his belly. He's what you might call portly."

"Fat, you mean."

"Oh, no! Philip makes too much money to be called fat." Her laugh tinkled between them. The questions darkening her beautiful eyes turned to a slow flame, tearing at his control. He couldn't let her go. Not yet. Not until he'd tasted her lips again.

His hand curved around her fragile neck, holding her. He felt her breath quicken, saw eagerness spread over her face.

He brought his mouth down hard on hers. Regan knew him now, the power of his arms, the firm demand of his lips. She made demands of her own, parting her lips to invite his tongue.

Everything faded—her fear of dying, the fact that they were strangers, her need to protect her fragile emotions.

Nothing in her life had ever consumed her like this need to get closer to him. It was primitive pure emotion feeding her.

She ran her hands up his arms to his shoulders. She did as he had done, framing his face. She went up on tiptoe, trying to get closer to that hard pleasuring mouth.

Cutter felt her strain toward him. He could take her now. On the bed, on the floor. It wouldn't matter. She wouldn't resist. Her defenses were down. The fire, the fear she was valiantly determined to minimize, her gratitude at finding she wasn't alone—those things had swept aside everything but the realization that she was alive, making her intensely vulnerable, more than even she knew. But he knew.

There wasn't a cop alive who hadn't received offers, and he'd turned down his share. True, sometimes it had been with regret, but even when he'd been single, he'd resisted the idea of victimizing a woman that way.

He couldn't do it now. Not when she'd made him feel alive again. Prison had taken almost everything he valued; he wouldn't let it take his honor, too. Even if she hated him now, she would thank him later. Days from now, if she happened to discover that her white-knight fire fighter had actually been an escaped felon, a convicted killer, she would be very glad he hadn't taken what she'd offered.

He dragged her hands from his face. She stared at him, her eyes nearly black with passion, her mouth parted and swollen from his. He pushed her away, holding her while she steadied herself.

"Jake?" The husky longing in her voice nearly broke his resolve.

He blunted his voice until it gave away nothing. "Find me those clothes. We've wasted enough time."

Was she wrong? she thought in a haze of desire. Hadn't his mouth taken hers like a man who was staking a claim? Hadn't his eyes grown fierce with hunger when he'd looked at her?

Now he stood staring down at her with a complete lack of interest. She'd seen that look before. In Tony's eyes, when he'd told her he was divorcing her to marry his pregnant mistress.

Hurt flooded her. Wouldn't she ever learn?

The need to protect herself made her lash out. "Do you always take advantage of the women you find alone and scared?'' she challenged. "Is that one of the perks of your job?''

Cutter went deadly still, his face cold. Guilt ground like broken glass in his belly.

"You're right,'' he said in a raw voice. "I'm out of line.''

Without another word, he moved her to one side, opened the door and stepped onto the porch.

"Where are you going?'' Regan asked stiffly.

"To see if I can get us out of this damned mess.'' He slammed the door behind him so hard the pictures rattled against the walls.

Regan flinched. She felt sick.

"Damn you,'' she whispered on a sob. "Damn you.'' She hated him for making her want him, for taking her to the very brink, for taking away her illusion that she was in control of her emotions.

She whirled around, looking for an escape from the hurt. But there was no place to go. She was trapped.

Cutter was a good ten yards from the porch when he noticed that the door he had slammed behind him an hour before was now ajar.

Ready to move quickly, he approached with silent careful steps. Habit made him keep his hands low, ready to defend himself from an attack that could come from any direction. Without seeming to, his gaze swept every inch of the porch and the open area in front of the cabin.

Something didn't feel right. Maybe it was the silence, or maybe it was the thought of the woman waiting inside that sent tension slicing down his spine.

He paused at the door and listened. Nothing.

Half expecting a man with a gun and shackles to be on the other side, he pushed the door wide, his body braced and ready, his gaze strafing the room.

Regan was on her knees in front of the cabin's only dresser. Her hair was pulled back from her face in a long thick braid, and she wore different clothes—bright pink sneakers, a loose white top that showed the smooth tan of her throat, tight cutoffs that cupped her bottom like fine leather. As soon as she heard his step on the bare floor, she stood up and turned to face him.

"Tell me there's a nice safe helicopter on its way here, and I'll be a happy woman."

With her hair pulled back, her heavily fringed cat's eyes seemed to take over her face. He steeled himself to accept the anger simmering there. They both knew he deserved it.

He kept his face expressionless. "No helicopter."

"But you said your crew would be looking for you when it was light."

"Forget my crew," he said. "They're probably history by now."

Regan saw the cold twist of his mouth and felt a swift stab of fear. She took a deep breath, then let it out slowly. "You mean they're . . . dead."

"Probably."

"You're . . . you're the only one who survived?"

Cutter shrugged. "I don't know. Like I told you last night, we got separated."

He closed the door behind him and leaned against it, folding his arms. The walk to the canyon rim had taken more out of him than he'd expected. He was beginning to feel light-headed, and his gut hurt like the devil.

Regan realized with a mental shudder that she'd never seen a man so unfeeling. All her life she had fought to help others. It was inconceivable to her that a man who made his living saving beautiful things thought so little of human life.

"Don't you even care?" she asked incredulously.

"Things happen."

Cutter spotted a coffeepot on the stove and a mug on the counter. Ignoring the shock on her face, he crossed to pour himself a cup. It was scalding hot and bitter, just the way he liked it.

Holding the mug in one hand, he rested his elbows on the counter and leaned back, taking some of the strain off the sore muscles of his belly.

Regan watched him lift his cup to his mouth. His throat worked for several swallows before he'd drunk his fill.

He caught her gaze on him and lifted his cup toward her in a mocking salute. "Better get yourself a cup before I drink it all."

She stared at him in disbelief. "You really are a cold bastard, aren't you?"

"Through and through," he drawled. "Take my advice and remember that."

"I feel sorry for you, Cutter," she said with real pity in her voice. "You must be a very unhappy man."

He felt the barb hit home. The last thing he wanted from her—from anyone—was pity. That she should offer it incensed him. He should have put on his clothes, wet or not, and kept on walking. That he hadn't been able to do that incensed him more.

"If I am, lady," he said coldly, "it's none of your damn business."

Regan's cheeks heated. "Regan," she shot back in an angry tone. "R-e-g-a-n. If you have to speak to me, use my name."

Knowing she was still watching him with angry eyes, Cutter took his time refilling his almost empty cup, then jerked his chin toward the neat pile of clothing on the bed.

"Those for me?"

"Yes." If she hadn't felt guilty about forgetting his wet clothes, she would have told him to take a flying leap.

She slammed the drawer shut and walked stiffly toward him. Turning her back on him, she poured the rest of the coffee into a mug. Her hands were shaking so badly she had trouble holding onto the pot.

"Okay, so there's no helicopter. I assume you have a plan to get us out of here?"

Cutter drained his cup and put it on the counter with a loud thud. "I'm heading south. I intend to walk until it's too dark to see my feet and then get up at first light and walk some more. If you want to come with me, that's up to you. I expect you to keep up."

"I'll keep up."

He cast a sardonic glance at her pink sneakers. "Look at you, with your pretty little designer shoes and fancy hundred-dollar cutoffs." His mouth flattened. "You're dressed for a stroll through some big city park, all show and no stamina. You'll be begging me to stop before we've gone five miles."

Regan sensed that he was more than angry. He seemed almost tormented, as though something brutal and unrelenting had an agonizing grip on him. Sympathy stirred, but she forced it down.

"You don't know me, Cutter, so I'll give you a little tip. I never say anything I don't mean."

Cutter thought about the promises he'd made in front of the priest with Elaine at his side. She'd made the same promises. He'd meant his. Hers had been designed to win herself a meal ticket.

"I've heard that from women before."

Knowing she'd just been insulted and determined to return the favor, Regan let her gaze follow the springy golden hair arrowing down his broad chest. Beneath the bruised flesh, his muscles tightened until she could see the tension rippling his skin.

"And I suppose you're dressed for mountain climbing."

"I would be, if little Miss Do-Gooder had left my damned clothes alone."

"Be glad I didn't wash your shorts, too."

He took a step forward, then winced as the movement sent vicious pain into his side.

"Damn Rhottman," he muttered, his breath coming in harsh gasps he couldn't control.

"Who's Rhottman?"

"Forget it."

Regan realized she'd pushed him too far. The man was half-dead from hunger and exhaustion. She put down her cup and reached for him.

"Here, hang onto me," she urged. "You shouldn't have gone traipsing around outside before you had something to eat."

Cutter felt a hand on his arm. Her fingers were cool, her touch gentle. He remembered the pity in her voice and jerked away.

"Save your energy. You're going to need it if you think you can keep up with me."

"I told you, I'll— What's that?"

She broke off, her head cocked toward a new sound intruding into the silence. A low droning, it rapidly grew louder until it filled the room. The walls shook, and her ears hurt.

"Oh, my God. A plane!"

She whirled and ran to the front door. She hurried to the edge of the porch, her sneakers making marks in the soot that covered the boards like black dust. The air was hot and filled with cinders. She looked upward.

The tanker was squat and fat, with bright orange wingtips and tail. It was flying low, only a few yards above the treetops, and coming directly toward her.

"Hello," she shouted as she raced down the steps and into the middle of the open space. "*Here*. We're here."

She waved her arms frantically, jumping up and down to attract the pilot's attention. The plane roared overhead, the rumble of its twin propellers deafening after the eerie silence.

"No, don't go!" she shouted after it. Even though she knew a plane that size couldn't land anywhere close, she didn't want it to go off and leave her.

Holding her hands over her ears, she watched it skim the trees to the south and head east toward the far end of the canyon. It circled, then dove, a long stream of something yellow billowing from its undercarriage.

Regan took the steps two at a time, raced across the porch and skidded into the cabin.

"Cutter!" she shouted. "The fire...a tanker. I waved, but the smoke was too thick. The pilot didn't see me."

Cutter had already seen it. They'd just run out of time. And he'd run out of choices. Fire was unpredictable, deadly. There was no way of knowing which way it would go next or how fast. Regan would be lost out there alone, out of her element, vulnerable. Like it or not, she was his responsibility now. Somehow he had to find a way to get her to safety without getting himself caught in the bargain.

"Jake, I'm scared," she said in a shaky rush. "I mean, really, *really* shaking-in-my-sneakers scared. I've never been in a forest fire before."

"The first thing to do is calm down," he said in the low commanding voice that had soothed countless victims and coaxed desperate men into laying down their weapons. "And then I want you to listen to me carefully."

She nodded her head, her gaze clinging to his. "I'm listening."

"Pack food and water, enough for three—no, make that four—days. Blankets, too, and a tarp if you have one. We're going to have to move fast, so think about weight. Don't take anything that isn't absolutely necessary. Okay?"

"Yes, food, water, blankets." Without wasting time on any more questions, she turned away and hurried back to the kitchen nook.

Cutter strode quickly to the porch, trying to get a read on the wind. It was stronger, but still from the east, he decided, shooting a quick look at the leaves rustling overhead.

So far so good.

Eyes intent and thoughtful, he studied the plume of smoke billowing skyward at the far end of Heartbreak Canyon. The canyon floor was serrated by sharp hills and valleys at least fifteen miles across. The steep walls were deep enough to add another mile that the fire had to burn before it reached the rim. He and Regan would head west, ahead of the flames.

He went back inside, leaving the door open. Regan was in the kitchen area, pulling cans and boxes from the shelves. Her cheeks were flushed, but her movements were quick and efficient.

He crossed to the bed, sorting quickly through the neat pile of clothing. There were shirts, underwear, socks, but no shorts, no trousers of any kind.

Without bothering about modesty, he stripped off his wrinkled skivvies, replacing them with a pair of dark blue briefs. The damn things were as snug as a jock, but they would have to do.

The shirt was almost as snug. If friend Philip was fat now, he'd been leaner once.

"Do you have a backpack?" he asked, turning around.

"No, just . . . just my tote." The startled look on her face told him that she was as aware of his body as he was of hers. He felt himself blush, the way he'd done as a kid with a crush.

Embarrassed as hell, he grabbed his jeans from the floor and began wringing the water from the dripping denim. Regan saw the sinews in his massive forearms bulge, and wondered if he was imagining his hands around her neck. He seemed angry enough to throttle her.

Hurriedly she opened the refrigerator and pulled out two large plastic bottles of mineral water. One was half-empty, and she refilled it from the tap.

"I don't have a canteen," she said in a rushed voice. "These will have to do."

When he didn't answer, she snuck a look over her shoulder. He had turned his back to her, as though he'd suddenly realized Philip's briefs had clearly outlined the decidedly potent evidence of his gender.

Looking at Tony had never made her go all hot inside. But then, Tony's body wouldn't have filled those briefs to bursting the way Cutter's did.

Hastily she returned her attention to packing.

When he couldn't force more water from the material, Cutter bent to pull on his jeans. A tight fit normally, they were even tighter when they were wet, and he wasted several precious seconds tugging them over his muscular thighs. His loins were still heavy with desire. The tight denim chaffed painfully.

"What's in the lean-to out back?" he asked, zipping his fly. He didn't waste time with the button of the waistband.

"The generator, some tools and things, uh, odds and ends. Philip's things."

"I'll check it out."

She heard him leave.

Regan turned and shot an anxious look through the open door. The cabin faced the wrong way. She couldn't see the flames, but she knew they were coming.

In her mind, she kept seeing the flames shooting out of the canyon right next to Rosie's bumper. She heard the roar and the rain of cinders hitting the top, felt the heat.

She shuddered, fighting down a sudden burst of panic.

Five minutes later, he was back, his arms full. He dumped the odd collection on the bed and began sorting through it.

Thank God he'd picked her cabin to collapse in, she thought as she carried a plastic bag to the table and began transferring the first-aid supplies from the heavy kit. Every few seconds she glanced through the broken window toward the canyon.

"Are we going down the road to Baker's Junction? There are some things in my car I should take. Papers in the glove box."

"We're going overland. There's a trail about ten miles west of here that leads to Tatum's Bend."

"But . . . Tatum's Bend. That's the direction the fire is going—west, I mean. Isn't it?"

"Yes."

"That doesn't make any sense. Shouldn't we go, uh, south? You know, where the fire isn't?"

"Regan," he said with restrained impatience, "the canyon is south."

"Oh, I . . . forgot."

Standing so close, Cutter could feel her trying to master her fear. He knew what it was like, struggling with terror. Something tore inside him. He wanted to drag her into his arms and comfort her, but he didn't dare.

He'd done three years in hell because he'd cared too much. He would never make that mistake again.

"Do you want to argue, or do you want to get the hell away from the fire?"

She saw the coldness return to his eyes. How could she possibly trust her life to a man like that, a man who kissed her as though he really cared, then deliberately thrust her away the way Tony had done? Yet what choice did she have?

She made her voice as cold as his. "I want to get the hell away from the fire, not that you care one way or the other."

She was already turning away when Cutter flinched.

Four

─────

Regan glanced at her watch. God help her, it was almost eleven. They'd been walking for three hours nonstop. Her legs felt like wood. Her lungs hurt. Her lack of sleep and the altitude were beginning to wear on her.

The smoke blocked out the sun, but the day was a late-summer scorcher. The lush greenery surrounding the cabin had been left far below. Now all she saw were drought-stunted pines and prickly brown bushes that tore at her flesh if she got careless and walked too near.

She risked a glance at the sky. Gradually the haze hanging over them had become thinner. Even she, with her limited hiking skills, knew they were angling away from the fire. According to her aching arches, they were heading straight uphill.

When she'd asked Jake why they had to go up before they could go down, he'd said something about skirting the canyon in order to give them an edge.

An edge.

At the moment she would sell her soul for five minutes' rest.

Wishing she'd had the foresight to bring sturdier shoes, she pushed her damp bangs away from her forehead and tried not to think about the miles and miles ahead of them.

"Thirty, thirty-five, maybe more," Cutter had said when she asked him before they left the safety of the cabin. That was about all he'd said. Other than to bark out orders, anyway.

"Take this. Don't take that," she mimicked, her voice coming out in harsh puffs. "You'd think the man was packing for an Arctic expedition."

In her tote, he'd packed soft things—blankets, the tarp that had covered the wood stacked alongside the house, the food that wasn't in cans or bottles.

In an old duffel he'd found in the shed, he'd stuffed the heavier things—the bottles of water, cans of food and an opener, even a rusty hatchet he'd found.

From the first step he'd set a fast pace. After a mile or so she had stopped trying to keep up. As long as he was in sight, she felt safe. Or as safe as she *could* feel with a forest fire at her back.

"I really detest hiking," she muttered, her gaze riveted on the middle of Cutter's broad back. Philip's polo shirt was plastered to his skin by the hot wind. His wet jeans clung to his legs, displaying every tough sinew and hard muscle of his thighs and buttocks.

He moved like a high-mountain predator, surefooted, unafraid of what might be waiting around the next bend. She wasn't certain why, but she knew he was intensely aware of his surroundings, like a man used to relying on his senses for survival.

She would want a man like that next to her at her side in a dark alley. Or, she realized with fleeting surprise, in the black of night when her memories pressed in.

Tough as he seemed, however, his injuries had taken their toll. He favored his left side where the bruise was the meanest. Now and then his head dropped forward and he staggered, but he didn't stop.

If he could keep walking, so could she. She'd made him a promise and, Lord help her, she would walk herself into total collapse before she would give him the satisfaction of seeing her breaking it.

She cast another glance over her shoulder. It was an act of paranoia, she knew, thinking the fire was right on top of her, but—

The toe of her sneaker caught on a half-hidden rock, and she stumbled. Her tote bag flew sideways, throwing her off balance, and she fell. Arms outstretched she landed heavily on one knee. Tears came to her eyes at the sudden jolt.

"Jake, wait!"

Cutter heard a scream and whirled, his body automatically going into a defensive crouch. He reached for his service revolver, only to remember that he was no longer entitled to carry one.

His gaze swept the path he had just traveled. Regan wasn't behind him. A clump of mesquite blocked her from his view. Pulse tripping, he took off running.

She was sitting on the ground, rubbing her knee. He squatted next to her, his hands braced on his thighs.

"What's wrong?" he demanded, his gaze sweeping over her, looking for injuries.

"I...tripped. I'm fine now."

Cutter ran his hand over her calf and ankle. Her knee was scraped and bleeding slightly. There didn't appear to be any swelling. At his touch, she stiffened and tried to pull away.

"Does that hurt?"

"No. Just my pride."

His gaze lifted to her face. Her cheeks were bright red, her skin beaded with moisture. Tiny ringlets stuck to her skin along her hairline and frizzed out from her braid. Her unpainted mouth had a weary droop that made her sultry lower lip seem even more enticing.

Why did she have to be so damned desirable? he thought with a silent growl of frustration. Half-dead and hurting, he still wanted her.

He brushed the dirt from the abrasion so gently she didn't even feel it. Regan tried to thank him, but her tongue felt thick and sluggish.

"You should be wearing jeans," he muttered, his voice irritable and tired.

"I told you, I didn't bring any." That's odd, she thought. She knew that she was speaking, but her voice seemed to be coming from a great distance. She was strangely woozy, as though her strength had suddenly drained away, and there was a terrible pounding behind her eyes. All around her the forest colors were slowly bleaching to white.

"I . . . feel funny," she mumbled. "Drunk."

Cutter placed two fingers against the pulse in her neck. It was pounding so fast he couldn't count the beats. His hand slid upward to cup her chin. The life had gone out of her eyes.

Cutter swore. "You're dehydrated. It's the heat and the altitude." He muttered a short pithy description of his own stupidity.

Regan tried to lean away from his big calloused hand. He wouldn't let her. "Swearing won't help," she murmured, trying to find a hint of warmth in those predator's eyes of his. "I know. I tried it often enough."

"Why doesn't that surprise me?"

"Beats me." A drowsy smile curved her lips and shimmered in her eyes.

Cutter slid his hand along her jaw, his thumb erasing a smudge of dirt from her chin. It took every hard-won ounce of the rigid control imprisonment had taught him to keep from accepting the invitation of those softly parted lips.

He said her name in his mind, but not aloud. He could almost taste the salt in the moisture shining above her lips. He could almost feel that soft impudent mouth move under his.

Almost.

He jerked his hand away. What the hell was he doing? The woman was half-dead, and so was he.

He found a water bottle in the bottom of his pack and twisted off the cap. "Take it slow," he ordered, handing it to her. Their hands brushed. As though burned, he withdrew his into a fist.

"Tastes good," she murmured between sips. The water was warm, but wonderfully wet against her parched throat. When she'd finally drunk her fill, she passed it back to Cutter, who put his mouth where hers had been and drank deeply.

When he spoke again, his voice carried an edge of anger. "Why the hell didn't you stop me?" Yelling at her was better than kissing her. At least he could control his anger.

Regan blinked at the swift change she'd sensed in him. Had she only imagined the slow melting of the ice in his eyes when he'd touched her? For an instant she had been sure he intended to kiss her. That thought both incensed and tantalized her.

"You have a way of not listening to me," she murmured, her voice still wobbly. "I have a feeling you don't listen to anyone much."

Cutter thought about the years he'd spent obeying orders from men he despised. "You're right. I don't."

He capped the bottle and returned it to the pack. He slipped her tote over his free shoulder and scooped her into his arms.

"I can walk," she protested. "Really."

"Right." His tone told her that he didn't intend to debate the point with her.

"Sorry," she mumbled. "I'm not usually this much trouble."

"Could have fooled me."

It took Regan a moment to realize that the unfamiliar note she'd heard in his deep voice was amusement.

"I don't believe it. You really do have a sense of humor." She stared disbelievingly at the stark lines and shadowed angles of his profile.

"Most people do."

"Uh-uh. Not you. You have to be human to appreciate the humorous side of life."

Because her eyes were only inches from his face, she saw the quick angry stretch of muscle along his jaw. "Don't push me, honey, or you just might find out how human I am."

"Don't push *me*," she mumbled. "You're the one who started it. You kissed me, remember? I didn't kiss you."

This time his jaw muscle bunched violently. "The hell you didn't!"

With every step he took, Cutter was more aware of the soft breasts crushed against his chest. Once he put her down, he would have to be careful not to touch her again. Otherwise, he wasn't sure he could stop until he was buried deep inside her.

She rested her head against the hard pillow of Jake's shoulder and thought about the man holding her. Big and rough, he was the most attractive man she'd ever met. His size, his powerful masculinity, his lean sinewy muscles, even the sweaty scent of his skin, made him appeal to her as no other man had ever done. She didn't like feeling that way. She just didn't seem to be able to stop.

"Regan?"

"Mmm?" Her lashes fluttered against his jaw as she tried to make her eyes stay open. Almost against her will, her fingers threaded into the thick hair covering his neck. For such dense hair it was surprisingly soft.

"Don't go to sleep. We can't stop for more than a few minutes. We need to put some distance between us and the fire."

Cutter headed for a patch of grass near a cluster of large rocks. Her eyes were closed, and her head was pressed into the hollow of his neck when he stopped.

"I'm fine," she insisted. "Just . . . need five minutes."

"Good. That's all you're going to get."

He deposited her on the ground with her back against one of the rocks. He lowered the packs to the grass and sat down next to her, careful to keep a foot or so between them. He retrieved the water bottle and twisted off the cap.

"Better have some more," he said, handing it to her. "Take a couple of aspirins, too."

She looked at him in surprise, her eyes reflecting the pale sky overhead. "How did you know I had a headache?"

He passed her the purple tote and watched while she rummaged around for the aspirin bottle. She was beginning to think he wouldn't answer when he said tersely, "I worked in the fields picking strawberries when I was a kid. It was piecework, so much a bushel. I ran out of water once and didn't stop to get more. It must have been over a hundred in the shade that day. I woke up in the emergency ward. It was a stupid macho thing to do, but I learned."

A man with his kind of lone-wolf confidence would have to learn life's lessons the hard way, she thought. How many of those scars on his lean body had come from such painful lessons?

She swallowed the aspirins and drank a few more sips before recapping the bottle. The wooziness was beginning to go away, but her legs still felt wobbly.

"Did you grow up in San Diego?" she asked, passing him the bottle. Talking was better than remembering the feel of his mouth sliding over hers.

"Yes." He stowed the bottle carefully in the duffel and leaned back against the granite. His dense lashes hid his eyes, his expression remote.

What was he thinking? Regan wondered. Two degrees in psychology and twelve years' working with all kinds of clients had taught her a lot about people. Her colleagues fondly teased her about being psychic. Philip claimed that she was so empathetic she could *feel* what people were really

like inside. There was some truth to both those things. So
why couldn't she read this man?

"Are you married, Cutter?"

She watched his hand slide down his thigh. She wondered how it would feel on hers.

"Divorced."

Jake didn't miss the sudden switch to his last name. He
understood her need to distance herself. Strange as it
seemed, he would miss the lilting twist she gave his Chris-
tian name.

"Any kids?" Regan drew her legs to her chest and rested
her chin on the knee that wasn't sore.

"One. Carole Ann. She lives with her mother and stepfather in Virginia."

Her polite smile warmed into an eager grin. "Tell me
about her. Does she look like you?"

She noted the slight hesitation before he answered, wondered about it. "More like her mother. Elaine is tiny, with
dark hair and eyes."

"Have you been divorced long?"

"Three years." He'd gotten the papers the first month
he'd been inside. Elaine had taken everything he'd had left,
even his beloved 1966 Mustang convertible. He'd been too
numb to fight her.

He opened his eyes and leaned forward to open her bag.
"We might as well eat lunch now. It's got to be close to
noon."

Regan was too tired to cheer. He hauled out two apples,
a banana, a box of cheese crackers and, finally, a bag of
peanut-butter chocolate miniatures.

"You'd better ration these," he said, tossing them into
her lap. "We're a long way from the nearest supermarket."

Her cheeks burned. Not from temper this time, but em-
barrassment. "Well, actually, there are two bags. I stuck one
in the duffel bag, too."

He shook his head. "You've got it bad."

Regan sighed dramatically. "I told you I was burned out. OD'ing on these helps put things back in perspective. They're a lot better than tranquilizers."

She opened the bag and offered him one. "Try it, you'll see."

He shook his head. "I hate the taste of chocolate."

Regan stared at him. He might as well have said he was here on leave from a Martian space shuttle.

"I gotta tell you, Cutter. I'm almost thirty-three years old, and I've *never* heard of anyone who didn't love chocolate."

Cutter was forty-two and knew that there were a lot of things she hadn't heard of. He hoped to God she never did.

"Here, eat this," he said, handing her a banana. "Just in case."

Regan grumbled, but did as she was told.

As they ate, Regan did most of the talking. Not by design, or even by choice. Cutter seemed to prefer it that way. He answered her questions with one or two words, then asked her four or five questions for every one of hers. After three or four times, she gave up. She interviewed people every day and was darn good at it. He was better.

To her surprise, he was also an attentive listener, as skilled at drawing her out as the therapist she'd seen for a few months after Tony had left her.

She found herself telling him about her rough-and-tumble childhood spent trying to keep up with four hell-raising brothers, about some of the sad lost children who made up her caseload, about the breakup of her marriage.

"I'll say this, Tony was a perfect gentleman about it. Took me to the best restaurant in the city, even plied me with vintage wine before he meticulously listed his reasons for choosing Mary Louise over me. Well, one reason, really. She could have babies. I couldn't."

Cutter felt a surge of anger. The man was a bastard and a fool. He would take Regan on any terms, he thought, and then froze. Three years of enforced celibacy was making him soft in the head.

"Of course, his timing left a lot to be desired," Regan plowed on, unaware of the sudden clenching of Cutter's hand on his thigh. "He laid all that on me the day I got out of the hospital after my miscarriage." Fiercely, she concentrated on unwrapping another chocolate. "He has his son now, and I hear Mary Louise is pregnant again. I wish her and the child well."

Somehow Cutter managed to keep his feelings pulled in tight. The longer he was with Regan, however, the more difficult that became. Maybe because she had a way of looking at him that made him want to tell her things he'd never told anyone before.

"You sound as though you've made peace with it."

"I do, don't I?"

She popped the candy into her mouth and let it melt on her tongue. When it was gone, the taste lingered, richly sensuous and addictive, leaving her wanting more—like she'd felt after Cutter's kiss.

"You should have seen me a year ago," she managed with a passable smile. "I was a mess. Every time I saw a baby, I'd throw up. Didn't matter if it was in the supermarket or at church or on the street. Once I nearly ran my TR, Rosie, into a parked car when I saw a mommy and her little one waiting to cross the street."

Because he couldn't handle the sad look in her eyes, Cutter picked up a bit of granite and pretended to study it.

"Sounds rough."

"It was." Her fingers weren't quite steady as they picked at the orange foil wrapping another candy. "I went through all the stages of grief. I mean, I wallowed in it. Seems I can't do anything by half measures." She took a deep breath. "So...so one day I parked my car on the scenic overlook by the Golden Gate Bridge and tried to find a reason not to jump."

He looked at her then. Eighteen years as a cop had taught him to watch the eyes. Hers, unguarded now, and pale green with anguish, told him she was telling the truth.

"Why didn't you?"

She ran her fingers through her bangs. "To this day, I'm not really certain. Maybe because I knew there was more to life than raising a child. Or maybe because I just got tired of feeling sorry for myself. In every other way, my life had been blessed. Why should I think I'm entitled to have everything I want?"

She shrugged, then smiled self-consciously. "What the heck, I just knew I couldn't give up that way. Not that I'm all that brave, because I'm not. You saw me this morning. When I saw that plane, I freaked."

Cutter couldn't let her beat on herself. "Fear of fire is one of the few things everyone carries in their genes. Like the drive to survive and reproduce."

"Then why aren't you afraid?"

"I am. I've just learned how to hide it."

The same way he'd learned to hide all his emotions, she thought with sudden insight.

"Thank you for that," she said quietly. "It helps."

He rested a burly forearm on his raised knee and stared out over the rugged terrain. "Elaine was pregnant twice. She lost the first baby. It was two years before she worked up the courage to try again."

"I would have done anything to have a child. I think that's in my genes, too. All those generations of Irish Catholics. My mom claims I was always a nester from the time I could walk. I do know I bullied my brothers into playing house with me until one by one they rebelled."

One side of his mouth moved up. "Carole Ann used to play house."

Sometimes he dreamed he was watching her rocking her beloved dolly, crooning the same lullaby he'd sung to her. Sometimes he could even hear her voice. Those were the worst times, when he woke to the obscenity of prison life with her sunny laughter still ringing in his ears.

"How old is she? Carole Ann, I mean?"

"Nine next month."

She smiled. "I'll bet she's a daddy's girl. Probably knows just how to twist you around her little finger, the way I did with my dad at that age." Lord, how her father had laughed at some of her more outrageous escapades before he'd kissed her small hurts all better.

"She doesn't know me. I haven't seen her in three years." He looked away from her, but not before she saw the quick tightening of his mouth.

"But, of course, you phone?"

"Not anymore."

Regan frowned. Was he one of those men who were fathers in name only? Disappointment ran through her. "But whyever not?"

Cutter wadded up the paper towel he'd used as a napkin and threw it into the duffel. "Elaine won't let her take my calls. She wants me to relinquish custody so that Carole Ann can be adopted by her stepfather."

"That's terrible!" Regan exclaimed with a look of outrage. "You're not going to agree?"

Cutter looked down at his split knuckles. "I haven't decided."

"Don't do it, Jake!" She scrambled to her knees and leaned toward him, ignoring the icy look of warning he shot toward her. "I see kids all the time who've been emotionally abandoned, kids from so-called good homes who end up on the streets trying to self-destruct, all because they believe their parents don't love them. You can't do that to your daughter."

His face froze, his shadowed eyes darkening to glittering bronze, his strong mouth taut. "I love her more than my life. I always have."

"Then, for God's sake, don't relinquish custody! Maybe you can't see her every day, but there are summer vacations, Christmas, spring break.'' Without thinking, she laid an urgent hand on his shoulder. ''As soon as we get off this mountain, get on a plane. Go see your daughter. Let her know you love her before it's too late.''

''Back off, Regan,'' he ordered angrily. ''My daughter is not part of your damned caseload, and neither am I.''

He jerked away from her touch and began shoving the remnants of their lunch into the bags. When he was done, he stood and shouldered both packs. When he turned to look at her, Regan had a sudden clear sense of some powerful emotion held in check.

''Jake, it's none of my business, I know, but—''

''You're right, Regan,'' he interrupted coldly. ''It's none of your damned business.'' Without waiting for her, he started walking.

Five

Cutter sat with his back against a fallen log, drinking coffee and listening to the hiss of the camp fire. The light was going. Long shadows stretched over the sparse meadow grass. The air had a bite to it now.

They'd made camp in a small rocky meadow surrounded by pines. While he'd chopped brush and built a fire, Regan had fixed a quick meal of stale peanut-butter sandwiches, overripe fruit and burned coffee. They'd eaten in silence, exchanging words only when necessary.

After they'd eaten, Regan had warmed a small amount of water and carried it to a grove of chaparral a dozen yards from the campsite. She was still there.

Cutter pulled up one knee, trying to ease the ache in his ribs. He was in a foul mood and restless as hell. He craved a cigarette. He craved sleep.

How long did it take to sluice off a day's grime? he thought irritably. Five minutes. Ten? He kept his gaze on the fire, trying to burn the image of her soft breasts and sleek tanned legs out of his brain.

Any woman would do, he'd told himself a dozen times since they'd stopped. A man in his situation wasn't choosy, he'd argued. Good reasoning, sound thinking—and complete unmitigated bull.

It was Regan who made him ache to hold her. Regan's voice he wanted to hear crying out his name. Regan's mouth he wanted to taste. Only Regan's.

Cutter shifted restlessly, wincing at the various aches and pains assaulting his tired body. Before he could stop it, his gaze went to the spot where she'd ducked into the thick chaparral. It wasn't as though she had a damned bathtub stashed in there, for God's sake. An inch or two of water was hardly enough to wet the tawny legs that were slowly driving him crazy. So what the hell was keeping her so long?

Cutter slugged down the rest of his coffee and tossed the plastic cup on top of the duffel. Two more days, he vowed grimly. Three at the most. And then he could drop her close to the logging road leading to Tatum's Bend and be on his way. No more pretending to be a fire fighter instead of a man on the run. No more pretending to ignore the hunger she put in him just by breathing.

In prison he'd learned to control his physical needs in the same rigid way he'd controlled his rage. Why the hell couldn't he do that now?

With a hard sigh, Cutter angled his tired gaze upward. Only a few stars were visible through the haze. The moon hadn't yet risen. The sky was soft purple tinged with black.

God, he'd missed the night sky. By this time of night he'd been locked in his cell. Even if he hadn't been, there were no windows in his cell block. No fresh air. No sunshine to warm a man's face. No rain splashing against a steaming pane.

Cutter inhaled against the bitter memory. How long would it take before he stopped feeling like a con? How long before he felt clean again?

A twig snapped to his right. He slitted his eyes and watched her walk toward him. She had changed into baggy shorts of some dark color and a white sweatshirt that looked soft yellow in the firelight.

Her skin was still dewy. The hair around her face was tousled and damp, framing her face with seal-brown curls.

Cutter ran his hand over his thigh, knowing that he really wanted to run his hand over her soft curves. He wanted to strip away that floppy shirt and kiss her breasts until they were slick and wet from his mouth. He wanted to plunge into her with his tongue, with his hard aching shaft, losing himself in her.

He felt desire arrow deep. He pulled up one leg to ease the pressure. It didn't help.

Regan tossed her dirty clothes into a pile by her tote bag. "I'll never take a shower for granted again," she said with a small tired smile.

"It's human nature to take things for granted—until you can't have something anymore."

Regan heard the tension in his voice and wondered what he'd taken for granted. "Your turn," she said, holding out the pan. A bar of clear complexion soap glistened in the bottom, still wet after sliding over her smooth tanned skin. "There's only one towel, I'm afraid. I left it hanging on a bush to dry. Feel free to use it."

Cutter grunted his thanks and forced himself to his feet. "The light will be gone soon. It'll be cold in a few hours. Better lay out your blanket close to the fire."

Regan nodded, her eyes shifting to the place where his bedroll lay on the other side of the fire ring, then back to his face.

"Oh, I almost forgot," she said. "I found a spare toothbrush and some toothpaste in the medicine chest. No razor, though. Philip has a full beard." She picked up her tote and searched through it for several seconds before coming up with the implements in question.

"Philip is compulsively prepared," she said, putting them into his outstretched hand. "Probably that's why he's a terrific trial attorney."

"What's his name?"

"Philip Emerson Sinclair. Ever hear of him?"

"Hasn't everyone in California?" Every cop in the state had reason to dislike the flamboyant San Francisco lawyer who routinely took only the toughest cases and won a fair number of them. Cutter had asked Sinclair to defend him at his trial. The man had refused. For philosophical reasons, his letter had said. Because he didn't like vigilante cops was what he'd meant.

Cutter thanked her and started to turn away.

She called his name, stopping him. "Uh, when you come back I'll dress that cut again."

Cutter wanted to tell her to leave him alone. He wanted to tell her to stop being so damned giving, so damned cheerful, so damned sexy. He didn't trust himself to say anything.

Instead he uncapped one of the water bottles and poured an inch into the pan. Some good those few drops would do, he thought as he walked toward the chaparral. He was dirty and sweaty and probably smelled like a goat.

Funny how a woman changes a man's perspective, he thought as he slipped between the twisted branches. In prison he hadn't given a tinker's damn what he looked or smelled like. He hadn't cared about anything but living long enough to get out. Now he was beginning to care too much, and that scared the hell out of him.

Ignoring the various aches and pains making his movements stiff and difficult, he peeled out of his clothes, throwing them on the dense screen of bushes.

He brushed his teeth, savoring the minty taste of the toothpaste. Wincing at the pain, he unwound the bandages from his hands and tugged the tape from his forehead. Then, exposed skin stinging in the chill, he took a quick infantryman's bath.

The water was cold. The soap stung the bruises on his face and smelled like Regan. When he was finished, he used the remaining water to wash the ash out of his hair.

Damn woman, he thought. A man could get lost in the web she wove with those big generous eyes and quick concern. Lost in thinking she would understand. Lost in believing she wouldn't care about the past. But she *would* care. What was it Elaine had told him? "No decent woman wants an ex-convict for a husband. She wants to introduce her husband to her friends, not be ashamed."

With a muttered curse, he grabbed the towel and dried his face and hair with hard angry strokes. He had no business wanting Regan Delaney. He threw down the towel and began to dress.

Regan was sitting cross-legged in front of the fire when he returned. She looked up when he approached, giving him a tired smile.

"When I was skidding straight for those awful flames, I swore I never wanted to see fire again," she said when he stepped into the light. "Now it feels awfully good."

"It'll feel even better in a couple hours."

Too tired to answer, Regan watched Cutter move past her, his boots dangling from his long fingers. He carried the pan in the other hand, Philip's borrowed shirt slung over his wide shoulder. His hair was damp and tousled. It was too thick to comb easily. From the looks of it, he hadn't even tried.

In the firelight his skin gleamed like polished oak. His chest hair was the same dark bronze as his brows and lashes, and curled softly against his skin.

How many women had fallen for that terrific body? she wondered as she watched him drop his boots and shirt by his bedroll and stow the pan in the duffel. How many had been determined to find out what had put the tormented look in those icy predator's eyes? How many had longed to see that hard mouth soften only for them?

Plenty, she thought. No doubt they'd been left sitting by the phone waiting for his call. It was something she would never do. It would hurt too much if the phone didn't ring.

"Are you all right?" His voice had a husky quality that surprised her. She looked up to find him watching her intently.

"Must be the fire," she murmured. "It's hypnotic." Conscious of his eyes on her, she hastily dug into her bag for the bandages.

"Sit down," she ordered as she got to her feet. "Let me take a look at that cut."

"A Band-Aid will do fine."

"Don't argue, Cutter. We're both too tired for that. You've lost a lot of blood because that cut isn't stitched. I'm going to try to close it with tape, so you won't lose any more."

Cutter had learned enough about first aid at the police academy and on the street as a beat cop to know that she was right. Steeling himself to accept her touch, he sat stiffly on the log and stared into the flames.

Regan took a piece of paper toweling from the roll and gently blotted away the blood that had begun to ooze from the gash again.

"This might hurt," she said with a hint of apology. Her fingers were warm, her touch gentle. Every movement of her arm caused the soft material of her shirt to slide over her breasts like a lover's hand.

Cutter scowled, the hunger in his gut clawing deeper. "Just get it done. I don't need the running commentary."

"Well, I do," she said in a testy tone. "It's too quiet here. I need . . . noise."

Try living with two thousand men and no privacy, and then you'll really know what noise is, Cutter thought sardonically.

Regan opened the bag, found the tape dispenser and tore off a strip about two inches long. "Give me your hand."

"Why?"

She leaned back to give him a chiding look that made him notice the way the fire put golden lights into her eyes. "For heaven's sake, Cutter, are you always this suspicious?"

The frustration gnawing at him made him forget his need to guard his words. "If I weren't, I'd be dead by now."

"You would? Why?"

Cutter cursed himself for being a fool. Half the cons in stir were there because they'd gotten careless. "Fires are unpredictable," he improvised. "I always suspect the worst."

"Well, you don't have to suspect the worst from me. I just need an extra hand, that's all."

Cutter took the dispenser from her hand. She must have applied lotion to her skin, because she smelled like flowers. He'd forgotten how good a woman could smell. He'd forgotten how it unsettled a man to notice such things.

He moved restlessly on the hard log. You're noticing too much, Cutter, he told himself angrily.

Regan blotted his head again, then applied the tape. Blood saturated the half-inch strip, and the end pulled loose.

"Rats!"

She took a slow ragged breath and reached for the towel again. She was just about at the end of a very long difficult rope. She tore off another strip of tape and tried again.

"You're going to have another scar," she said in a preoccupied tone. "I couldn't help noticing the one on your back. Did you get that fighting a fire?"

"No." He'd been sliced by a knife made from a plastic bottle. It had happened the first month inside. He'd half killed the guy, and no one had moved on him since.

"Have you been a fire fighter long?" Regan knew she was talking too much, but anything was better than the eerie quiet.

"Long enough."

"You don't talk much, do you?"

"Talking to you wears me out," he muttered before he thought. In stir, he'd gotten out of the habit of talking. Not

that he'd ever been much for conversation. Elaine had ac-
cused him of being dull. Hell, maybe he was.

"Sorry. I tend to chatter when I get nervous. Just ignore
me."

Cutter grunted. Her scent was seeping into his senses.
Even the soft timbre of her voice was getting to him. Damn,
he craved a smoke. Or a half dozen shooters of whiskey.
Anything to dull his mind and deaden the hunger for her
prowling in his gut.

With one hand still pressed against the tape she'd just
applied, she reached for another strip. Her breast grazed his
shoulder, and his body reacted immediately.

"Aren't you done yet?" His voice was barely controlled.
Sweat was beginning to trickle down the rigid line of his
spine and his head was throbbing.

"Almost." She caught her lower lip between her teeth and
frowned in concentration. Cutter thought about those soft
full lips moving under his. His patience gave out.

"That's enough, Regan," he warned in a low frustrated
growl. He felt like a damned teenager with a loaded pistol
in his jeans.

Regan plucked the roll of tape from his fingers and tapped
him on the shoulder with it. "There, all finished. You were
a good boy."

Cutter released the air in his lungs in a long stream. "Like
hell."

Regan laughed. "You're right. You're a terrible patient.
How about your hands?"

He extended them in front of him for a quick look.
"Healed up already." Enough so that it didn't matter, anyway.

Regan stowed the tape in the bag. Every time she moved,
it hurt someplace. With a small moan, she inched herself to
her bedroll and carefully crossed her legs Indian fashion.

"I'm so tired my eyelashes hurt, but I can't seem to make
myself close my eyes."

"Give it five minutes."

He got to his feet and stretched. In spite of his air of casual disinterest, Regan felt the pent-up energy in him. Even though he was standing still, she had the distinct impression that he wanted to prowl, like a large fierce animal put in too small a cage. No wonder he had chosen to work outdoors. A man as restless as he was would go crazy cooped up in an office. Even she sometimes felt claustrophobic in her small cubicle.

"I can't believe you're still on your feet," she said with an oblique look at his bandaged face. "Yesterday, when you passed out, I was afraid I was going to have to rescue you."

Cutter crouched by the fire to add another log. She would have tried, he thought. Not even knowing him or anything about him, she would have tried.

"Just how did you plan to do that?" he asked, keeping his gaze on the fire. One time, he thought. If he could have her once, the hunger would go away. He could stop thinking about those long legs, stop wondering how she would feel lying under him, stop aching.

"I had two plans actually. I believe in being prepared." She propped her elbows on her knees and rested her chin on her folded hands. "Plan A was to get you onto a blanket and drag you down to the place where my Triumph broke down. Then I was going to sort of drape you over the hood, like a...a moose, you know, and then let gravity roll us down the road to the rock slide."

That hooked him into looking at her. It was a mistake. The fire painted her face with exotic color, and her hair shimmered like gold. He'd never seen a more beautiful woman.

"A moose?" he managed to get out in a reasonably normal tone.

"Well, you're not exactly a lightweight, you know."

His eyes captured hers. She could feel herself being drawn to him before she remembered the look in his eyes when he'd thrust her away. This time she resisted, yet the temptation was strong. So strong.

"I admit, after that, the plan got fuzzy."

"And Plan B?" Cutter tossed another log on the fire. She was charming him, beguiling him, drawing him in. Why the hell couldn't he resist her?

"Promise you won't laugh?" Had she heard him laugh? she wondered, then realized she hadn't.

"That bad, huh?"

"Well, not exactly bad. Unorthodox, maybe."

Cutter poked the fire. With a loud crack, a shower of sparks shot upward, drawing her gaze. Beyond the flames she saw his face. Something was different about him tonight. He looked relaxed. She found that the possibility pleased her immensely. For some reason she had a feeling that relaxation was a rare experience for Cutter.

Her eyes danced. "Well, it's like this. I was going to climb up on the roof—"

"The hell you were!"

"—and spell out 'help' with my clothes and towels and things. Then—"

"You need a keeper," he interrupted in a half-teasing, half-irritated tone. "You know that, don't you?"

Regan couldn't hold back her grin. Was he applying for the job? she wondered, and felt an instant shiver of pleasure at the thought of being in Cutter's care.

"Then I was going to set fire to that big pine on that rocky place above the house. I figured it would serve as a torch."

"Hell of an idea," he muttered, lost in thoughts that had nothing to do with rescue, or even the fire. He felt himself letting go, smiling, even teasing—normal things a man did with a woman who appealed to him, things that were so removed from him now that he hadn't known he was doing them until he felt himself wanting to laugh.

"Don't you think it would have worked?" Regan prompted when the silence lengthened.

Cutter rubbed his palms over his knees. He was beginning to want her with a hunger that bordered on desperation. But nothing had changed. He still owed the state almost six more years of his life. More years than he was willing to pay.

"No," he said bluntly. "I think you would have broken your damn fool neck."

Regan's grin died, and her eyes flashed with hurt. She stared straight ahead, looking exactly like a woman who'd just been slapped.

Good, he told himself as he pushed to his feet. That would keep them both safe.

"I'm going to check the fire." Feeling sick, he walked into the darkness.

When he returned, he found her bundled into her blanket, the firelight gentle on her face. The walk had settled his nerves, but the need for her was still a hard ache in his belly.

"Any change?" she asked coolly when he settled down on his own bedroll.

"No. The wind's holding steady."

"Should we keep watch? In case the wind shifts again?"

Cutter lay on his back and folded his arms behind his head. "Keep watch if it makes you feel better. I'm going to sleep." He closed his eyes, shutting her out.

Regan turned onto her side, putting her back to him. She closed her eyes and pressed her knuckles to her mouth. She would *not* care about this man. No matter what, she wouldn't let herself reach out to him again.

The flames hissed and spat between them. Darkness pressed in. Somewhere to the north, the worst forest fire in California history still burned out of control.

Neither of them said good-night.

Regan awoke with a start. Her neck was stiff, and her head felt fuzzy. It took a second or two to orient herself. She was huddled into her blanket next to the fire, which was now little more than embers. The sky was a deep charcoal. Dawn would be breaking soon.

She sat up and looked across the faint glow of the fire. Cutter was sprawled on his back, one burly arm thrown over his head. Even in sleep, his features seemed drawn into hard lines. His breathing was harsh, like a man running a long punishing race.

As she watched, he turned his head away from her and muttered something in a low angry tone. He drew up one leg, moving restlessly, as though his dreams disturbed him. He groaned again, and the tortured sound made her wince.

"Jake?" she called softly. "Are you in pain? Is it your head?"

His face turned toward her, and he frowned. His gold-tipped lashes fluttered, but he didn't awake. He muttered something she couldn't understand, his voice rough with some terrible emotion.

Regan threw off the blanket and, teeth chattering and hands shaking, built up the fire. Should she wake him? she wondered as the fire began to take hold again. The last time he'd nearly put a fist through her face. No, she decided with a mental shudder. She wasn't ready to risk that again.

Arms crossed, she crouched by the fire, waiting for the flames to warm her. A shiver ran over her skin, adding to her uneasiness.

If this man had led an ordinary life, she was a trained bear. Something didn't add up. Not that she had anything against fire fighters, but Cutter seemed too savvy, too intelligent, to enjoy a life that was exclusively physical.

Sure, he seemed to relish testing himself against the fire, but there was an edge of recklessness about him that made her wonder how much he really valued his life. Cutter was a man touched by violence, that much was certain.

Was he addicted to risk the way some men were addicted to drugs or gambling? Or had he chosen to risk his life out of a desire to help others?

Having grown up surrounded by males, she knew a lot about men and what drove them. Sex, ego, a need to beat the competition. What drove Cutter?

Warmth from the fire gradually chased the shivers from her skin. Grabbing her tote and a bottle of water, she headed for the bushes.

Five minutes later, teeth brushed and sleep washed from her face, she returned to find Cutter thrashing from side to side, like a man struggling with a demon only he could see.

Regan dropped her things on her blanket and crouched next to him. He wasn't bleeding again, but he was clearly in pain. Beneath his closed lids his eyes moved constantly, as though he were on guard against someone or something.

Her mouth went dry. It would be light soon. She had to wake him. Careful not to touch him, she leaned forward and called his name.

"No," he mumbled. "Too soon."

"It's all right. You're dreaming."

He frowned, then slowly opened his eyes. Before she could curve her lips into a good-morning smile, he reached for her. His hand curled around her neck and pulled her toward him until she was lying across his chest.

He mumbled unintelligibly, his drowsy gaze searching for something in her face. His tawny eyes had an unfocused sheen, and she realized he wasn't really seeing her.

"Jake, wake—"

"Don't leave me," he whispered, as though she hadn't spoken, his voice hoarse with some private agony. Slowly, his other hand lifted to brush a tangle of sleep-tossed hair from her face. His hand was callused and hard, but his touch was surprisingly gentle.

"It's me. Regan," she said gently, laying her fingers against his whisker-rough jaw. "It's morning already. We don't have much time."

He didn't seem to hear her. His eyes turned dark, grew hungry. His thumb rubbed her cheekbone, sending tiny waves of pleasure over her skin until her face was wonderfully warm, and then his lips touched her lightly where his thumb had been.

Regan's breath quickened. She felt an eager flutter deep inside, followed almost immediately by a sudden light-headedness, which she did her best to ignore.

Her fingertips dug into his shoulders, and she tried to shake him awake. His flesh was solid and immovable, like the granite beneath the cabin.

He pulled her closer, his long fingers warm and possessive on the nape of her neck.

"Don't go," he whispered, his lashes drifting closed. "Not yet." His husky words had a tortured grittiness.

Regan stopped resisting and let him settle her against the hard pillow of his chest. She knew all too well the loneliness that came as sleep faded.

Beneath her cheek, his chest rose and fell in an agitated rhythm, like the erratic beat of her heart. Her breathing grew shallow. Her fingers stroked the sinewy length of his arm, trying to ease him from sleep.

A heavy sigh warmed her face, and his hands flattened against her spine, pressing her closer. Beneath her belly, she felt him begin to harden.

She sucked in a breath, her good intentions instantly supplanted by a rush of desire so elemental it shook her. Alarmed, she tried to escape his hold. As soon as she moved, his arms tightened, holding her immobile against his unyielding muscles.

"Jake, wake up!" she cried out sharply. "You're hurting me."

Cutter bolted upright, then winced at the hot stab of pain in his side. He blinked in confusion, his chest heaving violently as he tried to take in enough air. Regan lay tumbled across his legs, fear glazing her eyes. Her cheeks were red, her mouth trembling.

"God, I . . . what's wrong?" he ground out hoarsely.

Regan managed a shaky breath. "You were dreaming," she said, pushing herself to a sitting position. Her arms and legs were trembling. Inside, she was quivering. Her cheek was warm where his whiskers had scraped.

"Did I hurt you?"

Regan heard the remnants of his harsh groans in his voice. Whatever was driving him had been there in the dream.

"No," she said softly, feeling compassion well like unshed tears inside her. "Believe me, I'm fine."

That brought a quick stiff smile to his mouth. "Good." He couldn't quite keep the relief from his tone.

"But you did scare the bejabbers out of me," she added with an impish smile as she got up and wiped the dust from her legs. If she didn't diffuse the tension between them, they were both in for a long day.

Cutter got up heavily, feeling the weight of the suffocating nightmare pulling on him. His skin felt too small for his body. His blood felt hot. His muscles burned.

When he felt steady enough on his feet, he pulled a clean shirt from the duffel and jerked it over his head. Without looking at her, he pulled on his socks and boots. Then, straightening, he went to her.

His hands were gentle on her shoulders as he turned her to face him. His fingers were steady but tense as they softly stroked the scraped place on her cheek. "Did I do that?"

She nodded. "When I called your name, you . . . kissed me."

His hand eased the hair away from her neck, then rested on her shoulder. Regan felt the tension in him. "I didn't mean to do that. It'll only get us into trouble."

"Maybe I like trouble."

Cutter felt a moment of emotion so strong it nearly drove him to his knees. She couldn't care, she *shouldn't* care, but she did. About him, Jake Cutter.

But she didn't know him. Not really.

"Don't care about me, Regan," he said in a rough tortured tone. "I can handle anything but that."

Her finger traced the hard slant of his mouth. "It's too late, Jake. I already do."

With a tenderness he'd thought had been burned out of him, he caught her to him and buried his face against her neck.

Her arms went around his neck, and she snuggled close. Feeling her softness, smelling her scent, feeling her reach out to comfort him, made him long for her with a violence that shook him. He wanted to protect her and cherish her and grow old loving her. But it was too late for him.

Even if he made himself go back to serve the rest of his sentence, six more years in prison would destroy the small piece of humanity left in him.

Regan deserved a man who still remembered how to laugh, a man who believed in answered prayers and happy endings, a man who wasn't filled with bitter rage.

He raised his head and pulled away until he could see her face. Her skin seemed transparent, and her eyes were shadowed, her mouth pale.

He bent down to her slowly, watching her eyes begin to smile. Her breath sighed against his mouth, quickening his. His lips brushed hers.

"I'll take care of you," he said with a gentleness few had ever drawn from him. "For the time we have on this mountain, I'll keep you safe."

He allowed himself one more taste, one more brush of his hard mouth over the satin of hers, before he made himself release her.

"Now eat your breakfast," he said, when her eyes widened and her mouth parted. "We need to get the hell out of here." He snatched up his duffel and left her standing by the fire.

Six

———

Cutter leaned against the towering rock face leading to the peak. Six feet from where he sat, the ridge dropped away into the canyon at a dizzying angle. Behind and above them the fire sent smoke billowing into the sky, blocking out the sun.

It was midday. In spite of the haze overhead, the day was hot. They had been walking since early morning, working their way down the side of a steep slope leading to the valley floor. It had been hard slogging. In places the trail had been so narrow that they'd walked it single file, one foot directly in front of the other.

When he'd finally called a halt for lunch, Regan had been pale and breathing hard, and he'd been drenched in sweat. That had been an hour ago. Now she was asleep under a wind-twisted oak that clung tenaciously to the side of the rocky ledge.

He cut another slice of apple and slid it from the knife blade into his mouth. The moment it was rationed, fresh fruit was something he had found himself craving. Like a cold beer on a hot afternoon, or the fiery smooth taste of well-aged scotch after a long satisfying day. He cut another bit and crunched it slowly, savoring the crisp juicy sweetness.

Funny what a man missed in prison, he thought. A hot shower whenever he felt like it. A baseball game on a hot day at the stadium. The smell of newly cut grass. A woman's bubbling laughter.

Knowing he shouldn't, he slid his gaze to the right. Regan was curled on her side, her hands folded under her cheek. For the first time he noticed a splash of golden freckles over her small impudent nose. Her mouth was relaxed, the corners soft, her breath coming slowly and evenly.

Cutter snapped the blade closed on her friend Philip's Swiss army knife and slid it into his pocket. It wouldn't do any good to try to kid himself any longer. No matter how hard he pushed his body and hers, no matter how wrong it would be, he wanted to feel this woman lying beneath him, her body opening in welcome, her eyes glowing just for him.

In spite of the raging need inside him, he would make himself take his time, stroking her gently, kissing her into wanting him as much as he wanted her, undressing her slowly between heated kisses until neither of them knew anything but each other and the pleasure they were feeling.

Afterward... Afterward, what?

Would that be the right time to look into those innocent green eyes and tell her he was an escaped convict on his way to Mexico? An escaped killer?

What would he see in those eyes then? Horror? Fear? Revulsion?

He'd seen all of those things and more—in the eyes of the judge, of brother officers he'd thought were his friends, of the woman who had been his wife. No matter how hot and punishing the need grew inside him, he couldn't make himself accept those things from Regan.

Strung tight, he got to his feet and walked to the edge of the overhang. He'd chosen the quickest route, but also the most dangerous.

His sharp gaze traced the route they would have to follow, looking for problems. Fissured with pressure cracks, the footing was precarious in spots, making speed impossible. Quickly falling into old habits, his mind calculated the distance still to be traveled, tried to anticipate trouble before it caught them by surprise, sifted through possible dangers—all the things he'd done instinctively for so many years.

Feeling useful again, he raised his hand and tested the wind. So far it was holding from the west, but the fire was eating its way toward them. His best guess said it was still a day away, but the winds were unpredictable in summer. There was little time to waste.

"Regan," he called over his shoulder. "Time to go."

She mumbled something in her sleep but didn't awake. Cutter retraced his steps and crouched next to her. Her body was curled into a provocative curve, her breasts clearly outlined by a knit tank top. Her long slender legs stretched in smooth tawny allure below her shorts.

Cutter's mouth went dry. His hunger for her was like an ache, sharp at times, then growing dull, but always cutting into him. To his shock, he realized it was more than physical. Last night, this morning, somehow, the woman had gotten to him. He could have defended himself against just about anything but the one thing he'd thought he'd lost forever—trust.

For three years no one had trusted him. The bars that defined his existence reminded him of that fact every morning when he opened his eyes.

But Regan had trusted him from the beginning, even when he was bloody and dirty and waking up ready to slam his fist into her jaw. She'd been mad as hell, but still, she'd trusted him not to hurt her.

He slid his hand along her jaw, his thumb caressing the small red patch on her chin. He would die before he would let himself hurt her.

"Open your eyes, lady," he whispered.

"Mmm?" Her long lashes fluttered, and her lips curved into a drowsy smile. Waking was hard for her, this woman who went full out at everything she did. Would she make love with equal fervor? he wondered, and knew that she would.

"Jake?" she murmured, raising her head. "I ... didn't mean to fall asleep."

Her eyes were sleepy and shadow dark, her mouth close and inviting. The seductive lushness of her breasts was only inches from his hand. He felt his body tighten and swell. It would almost be worth the hell he would endure later to take her now.

"It's the altitude," he said, glancing toward the sharp peak cutting into the smoky clouds.

Regan sat up and pushed the unruly wisps of hair away from her cheek. She moved slowly, trying to ease the stiffness from her legs and arms. A quick glance at her watch told her that she'd been sleeping for over an hour.

"Fifteen minutes, no more," Cutter had said when they'd stopped to choke down another peanut-butter sandwich.

She angled a look at his tired face. The wheat-blond beard darkening his jaw did little to soften the savage harshness of his features. The bandage over his straight eyebrow was dirty, but at least he'd stopped losing blood.

"You'd be halfway down the mountain by now without me, wouldn't you?" she asked in a low voice.

Cutter remembered his harsh words, and guilt stabbed him hard. He'd been wrong about her. She wasn't cream-puff soft and pampered. She was out of her element, yes, but Regan was a fighter, just like him. She would rather drop on the trail than give up.

"I'm right where I want to be," he said in a low, tightly controlled voice. "For the first time in years."

The air around them grew still, Regan's breathing shallow. His eyes held a new expression. Softer, but with an intensity that hadn't been there before. She wondered what showed in her eyes.

"You said I was trouble."

"You *are* trouble. But not for the reason you think."

"So are you," she whispered. "Maybe we should leave it at that."

"Is that what you want?"

Her smile wobbled. She saw nothing but the hard masculine mouth so close to hers. "No."

Cutter fought a losing battle with his conscience. Nothing could have kept him from tasting that soft sweet mouth. With a silent plea for forgiveness, he bent and fitted his mouth to hers.

Regan inhaled, but the immediate shock gave way to a warm pleasurable need. His hard mouth was insistent yet surprisingly soft against her lips, coaxing her to respond with a skill that shook her.

One hand cupped her cheek, his long fingers threading into her hair, and the other rested on her shoulder, his palm flattened against the skin bared by the scoop neck of her top.

He was barely touching her, yet she could feel the male textures of him. The rough half-healed patches on his big square hand. The corded restrained strength of his arms. The firmness of flesh padding his massive shoulders. With a helpless moan of need, she laced her hands around his neck, her mouth eager for his.

Cutter stiffened, then in one lithe powerful movement pulled her to her feet. Tension corded his arms as they locked around her, forcing her against the powerful stretch of his long body.

He murmured something against her lips. A plea? Or was it a curse? His mouth hardened, grew hungry. A violent shudder ran through him. He crushed her to him, his mouth bruising hers with the force of his need.

Regan felt no pain, only a wild flare of answering need. Her body was suddenly swamped with feelings and sensations. Jake was making her feel like a woman again. Intensely valued. Desirable. Passionate. The lingering doubts Tony had instilled in her seemed faraway, like a half-remembered pain.

She ran her hands down the rigid strength of his long back. Her palms flattened, rubbing against his spine, trying to bring him closer. His body strained; his thighs went rigid. She felt his arousal.

His kiss was seductive, his tongue sliding into her mouth to explore, tantalize, enrapture. His hands moved over her, rubbing, stroking, feeding the fire inside her until she was consumed by it.

Her hands tugged his shirt free of his tight jeans, her fingers shaking with the need to touch his firm warm skin again. His body was solid, his muscles boldly defined, his shape fiercely masculine.

As soon as her hands moved over the puckered scar curving into the tight waistband of his jeans, he inhaled against her mouth.

"What's wrong?" she whispered in alarm. Beneath her fingers, she could feel him tense. "Does that hurt?"

"No," he grated, but she knew that it did—if not physically, then in some way even more painful.

Slowly, lovingly, her fingers kneaded the rough skin. With a harsh half-swallowed groan, he seared a kiss into her shoulder, his mouth moving over her skin with hot hunger.

Through the thin material of her shirt, his hand cupped her breast, his palm rotating slowly over the stiff nipple, drawing an answering moan from her parted lips. Threads of twisting demanding need spiraled deep, until she could no longer think.

He murmured her name in hoarse agony, and she recognized the question buried in the harsh sound. Lost in the rippling sensations shaking her, she started to answer, but the sudden angry clatter of a helicopter's rotor sliced through her breathless cry, tearing her from the sensual haze surrounding them.

Cutter's head shot up, his arms tightening protectively around her. The huge twin-rotored craft flew beneath the cloud that overcast the sky, angling south to north. Slung beneath the undercarriage was a bright orange metal basket containing fire-fighting chemicals.

Fear tore at her, making her oblivious to everything but the need to survive. With a strangled cry, she broke free and began running along the ledge in the same direction as the chopper. She slipped, righted herself, kept running. She heard Cutter's harsh shout, heard him begin to run after her.

Ahead was a triangular bulge in the narrow ledge, a spot without trees or brush to obscure the pilot's view, the perfect place to be seen. Thank God she was wearing a bright red shirt.

"Here!" she shouted, waving her arms. "Look down here!"

Just as she stepped into the open, Cutter's arm caught her around the waist, driving the wind from her lungs. He swung her around, away from the opening, away from the pilot's line of sight.

Adrenaline forced strength into her straining muscles, and she nearly broke free. Cutter's grip tightened until the pain bent her double.

"Stop fighting me!" he shouted, pushing her backward until her bottom hit the rock face. With one huge hand he pinned both her hands overhead, his body trapping hers. The thick umbrella of oak leaves screened them from view. In seconds it would be too late.

The racket overhead increased, echoing off the steep canyon walls to pound painfully through her head.

"They can't see us here," she shouted, trying to slip free of his hard grip. She squirmed against him, thigh against harder thigh. Soft hip against lean. He was as immovable as the granite rubbing her spine.

"Jake, can't you hear me? We have to get their attention."

The chopper moved past the top of the cliff. Seconds later the sound began fading.

Cutter released her and stepped back, long powerful legs braced, arms held loosely at his sides. His face was haggard, and he was breathing hard, as though the struggle had cost him.

But Regan saw only the empty sky where the helicopter had been. Fury heated her blood, overriding everything but the fear beating in her head as violently as her heart beat in her chest.

"Are you crazy?" she shouted. She was close to tears, and that made her even angrier. "Don't you know what you did? Don't you care if we die in this place? If this is taking care of me, I sure don't understand how!"

His face twisted, dusky color raging across his chiseled cheekbones. Quick as uncoiling steel, his hand curled around her wrist and he jerked her toward the clearing.

A hairline crack zigzagged crazily across the lip where she would have stood. His face savage with some brutal emotion, Cutter kicked down hard with his heel. That was all it took to send a four-foot section of ledge crashing five hundred feet straight down to the spiked treetops below.

"One more step and you would have been down there with those rocks," he hissed. "There wouldn't have been enough of you left to bury."

His straight dark brows drew into a hard line. Fierce golden eyes bored into her. For a heartbeat she thought she saw anguish there, stark and terrible—until he blinked it away. And then she saw no emotion at all.

Regan felt a constriction in her chest that wasn't caused by the thin air. Only a man whose emotions ran deep and strong could feel raw fear like that. But not for himself. For her. Only a man who had been unbearably wounded would fight so hard to keep it from showing.

Regan slid a sidelong glance toward the rocky abyss yawning in front of her. A shiver ran down her spine.

She took step toward him. Then another. "Jake, I—"

"Don't talk to me, Regan. I'm not in the mood."

He retraced his steps and began shoving things into his duffel bag. He worked quickly, efficiently, his movements rigidly controlled, like a man pushed to his limit.

He stood, hefting his duffel to one shoulder, her tote bag to the other. Before he could move forward, she stepped into the path, blocking the only way down.

His face closed. His eyes went cold, but Regan wasn't afraid. Not anymore. She knew him now, instinctively, intuitively, better than he thought she did.

Nothing about Cutter was gentle or easy to understand. Hardness and compassion ran side by side in him. Touch him deeply, and he would react—sometimes lashing out, sometimes bleeding in some private part of him. But he had been there when she needed him.

"I didn't mean what I said," she said softly. "I have this temper.... I know you care about me. I can feel it, and I'm never wrong about those things."

Cutter felt something slam into his gut, something that hit hard and twisted deep.

Lies. Betrayal. Humiliation. Indignity. He'd lived with all of them, and they'd lashed him until he'd felt raw and bloody inside. Why did the truth hurt even more?

Because he couldn't give in to it. Because he would only end up hurting her. Because hurting her would do what loneliness and humiliation and suffocating claustrophobia hadn't done. It would break him.

Digging deep for the strength to do what he needed to do, he said in the same cold tone he'd used with Rhottman, "Stay close. The next time you do something stupid, I might not be so quick to save your cute little butt."

For a moment, when her smile wobbled and her eyes widened into hurt, he nearly relented and hauled her into his arms. Only his iron will, forged in prison's terrible fire, saved her.

Before he could change his mind, he shook off her hand, shouldered her aside and started walking.

They walked steadily all afternoon, stopping only once for water and a short rest. Cutter said little. Regan said even less. Instead she concentrated on walking where he walked. He set a brutal pace, using long angry strides, as though he couldn't get away from her fast enough.

He seemed tireless, moving with surprising grace for so big a man. Regan found herself blindly watching the play of his back muscles against the sweat-dampened material of his shirt, so numb with fatigue that she could only feel, not think.

The strength she'd gathered from her short nap had long since disappeared. Her throat was so dry that it was agony to swallow, and her feet were sore and aching, but she refused to ask him for a rest. No matter what he had said, she knew he could travel much faster without her, might already have reached safety.

She was so preoccupied with putting one foot in front of the other that it took her a moment to realize he'd stopped walking and was waiting for her to catch up.

Regan straightened her stooped shoulders and tried to mask her limp with a faster pace. At the moment she didn't care about anything but getting off her feet.

"We'll camp here tonight," he said, watching her with that alert still-as-death gaze, which missed nothing.

She was so tired that she could only manage a nod.

Cutter felt guilt twist the knot in his belly tighter. He was nearly half-dead himself, but the punishing pace had been necessary.

If he'd been alone he would have pushed on until he fell in his tracks. But Regan needed rest. He had to risk stopping.

"I'll make the sandwiches tonight," he said when she caught up to him. "You go soak your feet."

Regan blinked up at him, certain she hadn't heard him right. "Is . . . is that a joke, or another insult?" she managed with a half-hearted smile.

"No joke. Follow me."

Turning, he walked past the mesquite, but not before she noticed that most of the tension had drained from his face. Enough remained, however, to remind her of the hard angry man who had warned her off. She wondered whom he was protecting so savagely. Himself? Or her?

The thought intrigued her. Later, when she wasn't so tired, she intended to think about it. She might not come up with an answer, but thinking about Jake was better than lying awake in a cold sweat, hearing the fire's approach in every sound.

Regan allowed herself a slow tired stretch, followed by a ragged sigh of relief, then trudged after him.

Beyond the gnarled stand of trees a pine-fragrant meadow opened on three sides, as flat as the trail had been steep. A stream meandered through the clearing like a crumpled ribbon of shiny metal. In spite of the year-long drought, clear sparkling water ran nearly a foot deep over the rocky bottom. Thick green grass grew along the banks, bright scallops of color in the sparse brown landscape.

"Is it real?" she whispered, not quite believing her eyes.

Cutter's hard features seemed to soften for an instant before he tossed off her words with a shrug. "It's real."

"Can I get a drink?" she asked eagerly. "I mean, is it safe?"

Nothing is safe, my sweet innocent, he wanted to tell her. Not even me. "It's safe."

Regan walked to the stream and sank onto the velvet grass. Ignoring the ache in her back, she leaned forward and scooped water into her mouth. Drops splashed her face and ran down her neck.

Closing her eyes, she drank her fill, then splashed handful after handful over her dusty face until the numbness began to dissolve.

Meanwhile, Cutter dropped the packs near a small cluster of chaparral and rock, then found his own spot by the stream and drank deeply.

Bending, he used both hands to sluice water over his head and neck. The water soothed his bruises but did nothing to ease the burning just below the surface of his skin.

On the ridge, when he'd kissed her, he'd felt the hunger in her response. He'd bedded enough women to know that she had wanted him. If he found that logging road tomorrow, this might be their last night together.

"This is heaven," Regan murmured when he raised his head again. "I'd kill for a bath."

Cutter stared at the rippling water. Instead of his own image, he saw Regan stretched out in front of him, her supple body wet and slick. He thought about tiny drops of water beading on the swell of her breasts, joining together in a thin line, sliding slowly down the satiny skin between her breasts, down the sleek curve of her waist to her belly, moving lower like drizzled honey. He thought about following that slow-moving drizzle with his tongue.

Blood pooled with fierce heat in his groin. Only the tight fit of his jeans kept his arousal from becoming embarrassingly obvious.

With a silent mad-as-hell groan, he pushed himself to his feet, every muscle and tendon screaming.

"I'm going to check the wind," he said with an impatient glance toward the steep rise to the northwest. "I'll be gone at least twenty minutes, probably more. Take your bath. It'll be your only chance."

Seven

Regan balanced Philip's duffel on the large flat rock she'd
selected as a table and began removing food for their meal.
Her hair was still damp from her bath, and her skin felt
wonderfully clean and cool. A long soak had taken most of
the tiredness from her muscles.

Cutter was a few yards away, cutting wood for the fire
with Philip's hatchet. His chest was bare, his hair damp and
smoothed back from his face after the bath he'd taken soon
after returning.

"We have peanut butter and jelly," she said, hauling out
one jar, then another. "Or, let me see here, jelly and peanut butter. Which would you prefer?"

Cutter glanced over his shoulder. In the fading light his
whiskers looked more brown than blond, giving him an
outlaw harshness she found more exciting than frightening.

"You choose. You're the cook. I'm just the grunt labor."

Regan grinned. The longer they were together, the more his personality seemed to unfold. And the more she saw of the man inside, the more drawn to him she became.

"Right. We'll have peanut butter and jelly. And bananas. If you want, I'll slice them into your sandwich, the way I do mine."

"God help me," Cutter muttered, sending the hatchet blade deep into a gnarled clump of chaparral. Tired as he was, the physical activity helped keep his mind off the woman who was going to be sleeping next to him in just a few hours. Next to him, but not with him, which was the way it had to be.

Regan heard the caustic note in his voice and threw him a dry look. "Trust me, it's a gourmet delight. I practically lived on peanut butter and bananas in college."

"Oh, yeah? Well, I ate roasted monkey in Vietnam. Trust me, it was god-awful, but this sounds worse."

Regan laughed and began laying out slices of bread on a dish towel she was using as a tablecloth.

"My oldest brother was in Vietnam," she said with a quick nervous look at the growing darkness. "He was a navy flyer. How about you?"

There was a moment's pause before he answered. "Infantry. The 196th."

Cutter carried a stack of wood to the pile by the fire. He fed two logs to the flames, then watched them catch. Even then, he was aware of every move Regan made.

He'd returned from the stream to find her bustling around like a woman afraid to stand still. He understood that very well. Activity kept a person from thinking too much.

At Donovan he'd played basketball, a game he hated, because it tired his muscles and kept his mind off his surroundings.

Slathering peanut butter on thick, she said, "Something tells me you were an officer."

"What makes you say that?" Cutter wondered if she knew how appealing she was with her hair piled on top of her head in a slapdash tangle of curls, and a teasing smile curving her lips.

"Because you act as though you're used to being in charge."

One side of his mouth moved. Was he agreeing? she wondered, or remembering the orders he'd barked out from the moment they'd met. "No officer. I was a sergeant when I got out."

Regan finished the sandwiches and began rummaging in the bag for their one cooking pot and the jar of instant coffee. "You sound like you have something against officers."

"Not anymore."

Taking up his hatchet again, he headed for a thicket of dead mesquite. As he reduced the wrist-thick logs to campfire length, he thought about the woman who'd doggedly walked in his shadow hour after hour.

All of this was brand-new to her, strange, most probably intimidating, and yet she was trying to make jokes. Admiration stirred in him, adding to the long list of things he was beginning to feel about her.

"All ready," Regan called, glancing his way. Every time she looked at him, he felt vulnerable, as though any minute she would remember his name or the endless detailed reports that had been in the paper day after day.

He wasn't much for analyzing his feelings—hell, he didn't even want to feel anything anymore—but suddenly he realized he didn't want the warmth in her eyes to fade or the soft smile curving her lips to disappear.

Cutter sank the blade of the hatchet into the dead log and started toward her. It had been so long since he'd eaten that he was light-headed. Whatever she made, he would eat and be glad to get it.

Regan stood by her table expectantly. Everything had been laid out neatly, using paper towels for plates and plastic cups for coffee mugs. They were running out of supplies, but then, they were also running out of time.

"Very nice," Cutter said, because she'd gone to so much trouble.

"Oh, wait. We need a centerpiece." She looked around quickly. "Pinecones!" Her eyes lit up, and she walked past him to a pile of rocks and dirt near the log.

Cutter stopped, staring at her with his hands balled on his hips. "What?"

Regan flashed him a tired smile, then began gathering the small brown cones scattered near the root end of a fallen Douglas fir.

"A centerpiece. You know, for ambiance."

"Ambiance? Are you nuts? You're dead on your feet, and you want a centerpiece?"

"Hey, I'll have you know this is a class restaurant."

Cutter was still alive because he knew how to read people, the look in their eyes, their body language, the things they didn't say. But, for the life of him, he couldn't predict what this woman was going to do next. That made her dangerous. It also made her damn near irresistible.

He stood silently and let himself enjoy the sight of her round firm bottom as she knelt on the ground, holding the cones in the tails of her shirt.

"Don't wait for me if you're hungry. I just need a few—" She froze with a soft cry of shock, her hand stretched toward a perfectly shaped cone caught between two rocks. Less than a foot away, a timber rattler had coiled itself against a large chunk of limestone for warmth, its tawny colors blending into the dirt beneath its thick body.

As soon as Regan had unknowingly reached toward it, the snake had tightened its coil and angled its head for attack. It's tail began to rattle an ominous warning. Stretched in an awkward position, she couldn't move without drawing the snake's strike.

"Easy," Cutter said in low steady voice. "Stay calm. If you don't move, he won't, either."

His intense gaze focused on the snake's slitted yellow eyes, Cutter edged sideways until the fingers of his left hand closed around the handle of the hatchet.

"Hurry. It doesn't...like me." Her voice was shaking so hard she wondered if Cutter understood her words.

Her eyes were welded to the snake. She saw nothing but the ugly flat head pointed directly at her arm, heard nothing but the angry rattle of its surprisingly fragile-looking tail.

Panic nipped at her. She couldn't hold still. She—

Cutter moved so quickly that she saw only a blur. With one swift powerful swing, Cutter chopped off the snake's head.

Regan stared at the thick headless body still jerking as though it were alive, her scream echoing over the hills. The blade of the hatchet was embedded in the hard dirt, the handle smeared with blood where Cutter had gripped so hard that the half-healed blisters on his palm had split open.

With pinecones spilling to the ground and piling around her feet, Regan launched herself against Cutter's chest, her arms wrapping around his neck.

His arms tightened. He felt the shudders rip through her slender body, heard her quick gulps of terror. "It's all right," he murmured, calming her the way he used to calm his daughter after a bad dream.

He cradled her tightly, fiercely, his body absorbing the tremors from hers. He held her without speaking, letting the silence drift down around them.

Eyes closed, Regan rested her cheek against Cutter's shoulder. Slowly he began combing her almost dry hair with his fingers, the movement of his big strong hand hypnotically gentle. Her tremors lessened to an occasional shiver.

She heard the trickle of the water over the rocks, the hushed sound of their mingled breathing. The smoke-scented breeze caressed her bare skin.

"Better now?" he asked some moments later.

Regan felt a slow spiral of desire begin to uncoil in warm secret places inside her. She leaned away from him and nodded.

"You make me feel so safe," she whispered.

Cutter captured her hands with his. He was close to the edge, just holding her.

She raised her gaze to his. "What do I make you feel?"

He dropped his gaze, then raised it. The pain in his lonely eyes nearly staggered her. "I don't know feelings, Regan. Not anymore. I just know I can't make myself resist you, and that scares the hell out of me."

Framing her face with his hands, he brought his mouth to hers slowly, giving her time to stop him. Her eyes widened, but the resistance he expected was missing.

The touch of his mouth on hers was softly seductive, drawing a breathless sound of pleasure from her parted lips.

Hunger ripped through Cutter's tired body, nearly overriding his forged-steel control. He longed to slide his tongue between lips slick from his kiss, to taste the wild sweetness that was her mouth, to ease the ache of loneliness inside him. But his restraint was stretched almost to breaking. He had no confidence that he could stop at just a kiss.

He raised his head and released her. "Walk away, Regan," he ordered tautly. "I'm no good for you. I'm burned out, used up, cynical as hell. Even if I wanted to give you what your eyes tell me you want, I can't. I'm empty inside."

He sounded so desolate, so alone.

Regan knew suddenly that she loved this man. In some basic instinctive bonding she couldn't begin to understand, he was hers, and she was his.

Feeling bolder than she'd ever been with a man, than she'd ever wanted to be, she traced the uncompromising line of his mouth with her fingertip.

"This might be my last night on earth," she whispered.

"We'll make it," he said. "I won't let—"

"Shh," she said, placing two fingers against his hard mouth. She knew her own mouth was soft, willing, eager. She felt vulnerable, open to him. Her smile trembled. Her breath grew shallow.

"I'm not being melodramatic, just realistic. I'm not saying I'm not scared, because I am. And, God knows, I don't want to die. But I also don't want to waste this night." She wound her arms around his neck and started to bring her mouth to his.

He stopped her by placing both callused hands on her shoulders.

"You'd better make damn sure you know what you want, Regan. If you kiss me again, I won't stop until I'm inside you." As though to emphasize his meaning, he pulled her against him until she could feel the hard bulge of his need.

Regan experienced a moment of terror. What was she doing? Her body and her emotions were intimately entwined. She would be making love. He wouldn't. Could she bear it when he walked away?

She looked into his face. Into his lonely eyes. No man had ever wanted her the way Cutter wanted her. No one had ever needed her as badly as he needed her at this moment. That was enough.

"I want you, too." Her voice was as whisper soft as the breeze caressing them. No matter what happened, she would have tonight.

His hands threaded through her hair, his thumbs angling her face to his, holding her immobile. His gaze roamed her features, his brows drawn into a savage line, his mouth grim.

"Tonight you're mine," he whispered hoarsely. "No past, no future. Just the two of us."

Regan felt a sad smile form in her mind. In his own blunt way, he was warning her not to expect more than tonight. "Just the two of us."

With a harsh groan, he brought his face down to hers, taking her mouth with the blunt aggression she had come to associate with him.

His tongue was hotly seductive, plunging deeply, then withdrawing to tease her lower lip. His hands roamed possessively, sliding downward to cup her buttocks, lifting her even more intimately against him.

She felt possessed, wooed, cherished. "Yes," she whispered. "Oh, yes."

His kisses ceased, and he stepped back, his hands going to the front of her shirt. One by one he worked the buttons until her shirt hung open, revealing the swell of her breasts. In the fading light the small nipples were rosy dark against the smooth cream of her skin.

So slowly that she felt herself holding her breath, he bent to touch his tongue to each dark peak, making her gasp with pleasure. His breath was warm and moist, his mouth gentle. She clung to his shoulders, her fingers digging into his naked flesh.

Cutter moved upward, trailing kisses along the satin warmth of her skin to the hollow of her throat. When his tongue found the pulse beating furiously there just for him, he couldn't contain a ragged groan.

Years and years of loneliness closed in on him, making him shake. Clenching his jaw, he made himself wait, made himself resist the urge to throw her down now and thrust deep and hard until he no longer hurt.

When he had himself under control again, he began to undress her, taking his time. His strong capable fingers pushed the shirt over her shoulders, down her arms. He released the button on her shorts, then the zipper, slid them down her thighs until she stood before him clad only in thin bikini panties, her clothes in a puddle at her feet.

His eyes flashed and his breathing stopped. He looked at her as though he had just found something precious after a long painful search.

"God help me," he whispered in a husky voice that wasn't quite steady. "Perfect doesn't begin to describe you."

His hand slid against her cheek, drawing her to him for a reverent kiss that brought tears to her eyes. Never had she felt so enticing, so deliciously feminine, so deeply cherished.

Suddenly he bent and lifted her into his arms. She clung to him, her face pressed against his strong brown neck. She heard the ground crunch under his boots, felt the lithe strength of his muscles moving beneath her.

Then he was letting her slide down his body. Her bare feet touched the rough wool of the blanket, the fire warm on her bare skin.

He stepped back, removed his boots and socks, then slowly straightened, his gaze flowing over her with a reverence that stole her breath.

He reached for her, his hands molding her waist, his fingers massaging her spine. She closed her eyes and gave herself up to the pleasure flowing like four-star cognac in her veins.

One hand held her, while the other moved lower, sliding over the thin material of her panties to caress the soft mound between her legs.

Pleasure pierced her, drawing a low moan from her lips.

"Good?" he whispered against her mouth.

She answered him with another moaning whimper. His fingers dipped beneath the silk to the soft whorls of hair hidden there.

He stepped back, drawing an urgent protest from her lips. His face was drawn into tense lines, his mouth half-open to ease his tortured breathing.

His hand shook visibly as he unzipped his fly. Regan felt a wave of anticipation run like hot caressing fingers down her belly. She held her breath, afraid to look, unable not to.

Cutter watched her as he rid himself of his jeans, his eyes glittering in the dim light, his expression hungry. Released from the heavy material, his arousal thrust toward her, hard and rigid.

He drew her down to the blanket and began kissing her. Her hand began to move, running over his shoulders, into his hair.

He seared a kiss into the sweet-smelling skin of her shoulder. At the same time, his hand molded her breast. He felt it swell against his palm, engorged with the same need punishing him. He knew he was close to losing control.

He held his breath, his gaze devouring her as his hands slid her panties down the sleek thighs that had tortured him for days. His heart began thundering in his ears.

Regan gasped as the cool air caressed the mound his touch had heated. When his hand slid between her legs, she began tossing her head from side to side, trying to escape the exquisite pressure building in her. Her skin was on fire, her eyes closed, the feathery lashes that fascinated him quivering sensuously.

With each stroke of his fingers, she became more frenzied. She arched toward him, the rapture on her face making him shake. She was his, this remarkable, strong, adorable woman.

Tendons distended in an agony of control, he settled into the cradle of her legs gently, letting her take him inch by inch until they were fully joined.

Regan gasped again, a long shuddering cry that traveled the length of her body. Her hands raked his back.

His control snapped. He plunged into her, savage need shuddering through him with as much potency as pleasure. She resisted nothing, answering his thrusts with wild cries that he caught with his mouth.

Regan was lost, awash with heat, her body pulsating with the greatest pleasure she'd ever known. She thought nothing, felt everything. Pure sensation, pure pleasure—building, building, until there was nothing but a blinding explosion of exquisite feeling. She cried out, saying his name, other words.

Cutter saw the rapture take over her face and closed his eyes, taking the image with him as he thrust deeply one more time.

His release was cataclysmic, shaking him to his soul. But ever more shattering were the words she had uttered.

"I love you."

The sky above was a soft shade of charcoal. A dozen yards away, the stream trickled over the rocks. The air was still.

Cutter lay on his back, cradling Regan against him. She was curled like a lazy cat into the warmth of his body, her hair tumbling against his neck and one slender leg thrown over his thigh. One hand was tangled in the hair on his chest. Her soft even breathing told him she was asleep.

Using his free hand, he reached out to pull the blanket over their naked bodies, more for warmth than modesty. As the wool slid over her bare skin, her long lashes fluttered, and she mumbled something in a contented tone before rubbing her flexed knee against his tense muscles as though trying to find a softer mattress.

"Mmm. Jake?"

"I'm here," he whispered before brushing a kiss across her temple. Soon he would have to let her go. For her own good. For his.

She snuggled closer, her breasts sliding over his muscles in provocative little movements. Cutter drew a breath quickly, his body beginning to stir. Knowing he shouldn't, he nudged her chin higher until he could brush his mouth over hers.

"Sweetness," he whispered against the slow curve of her smile. "Open your eyes."

"If I do, will you stop kissing me?" she asked in a throbbing whisper, her lashes still resting on her cheeks.

"Little tease," he said, his throat so tight he had trouble saying anything at all.

Twining her arms around his neck, she kissed the stern mouth that should smile much more often, then nuzzled her forehead against his stubbled jaw. It was true, she thought with happy amazement. She loved Jake Cutter. She had a feeling she'd loved him from the moment his head had dropped against her shoulder and his arms had tightened around her as though finally, after a long terrible journey, he had come home.

"You're scratchy," she said with a laugh. She ran her fingers over his jaw, expecting him to smile. When he didn't, she felt some of the bubbling happiness inside her start to slip away. "Have you ever had a beard before?"

"No." He tried to return to the icy numbness that had kept him sane. He couldn't want the things she was offering, but every time she touched him, he found it harder to stay removed from her.

"Why not?"

The San Diego Police Department didn't allow them. "Never wanted to, I guess."

She tilted her head and studied the angular lines of his face. She thought he was gorgeous with a beard, and then wondered immediately what he would look like clean shaven.

"Take it from me, it's very sexy. I love—"

With a sudden powerful motion that brought a squeak of surprise from Regan, he lifted them to a sitting position, his arms keeping her from falling. Her hair cascaded in a glossy wave down her back, feeling like cool sensuous silk against his arm. She fit perfectly in his lap, her soft breasts pressed against his chest, her mouth in the precise position to meet his kiss.

"Very nice," she said. "Something tells me you've had a lot of practice at this kind of thing." And I hate the idea that you've made love to other women before me, she added silently.

"Regan, stop talking a minute."

"You don't have to yell," she said in an offended tone. "I can't help it if I talk too much when I'm happy."

Happy. Cutter felt guilt tighten its claws in his gut. He had to put an end to this before she really started to believe the words she'd cried out.

He slid her from his lap and got to his feet quickly, before he could change his mind. Without looking at her, he grabbed his jeans. He jerked them over his legs and zipped his fly.

"What's wrong?"

"I made a mistake."

"Jake, talk to me," Regan pleaded. "Tell me what you're feeling."

"Nothing. I'm feeling nothing." She heard a deeply buried whisper of pain in the clipped cold words.

She dropped the blanket and stood. It never occurred to her to feel embarrassed about her nakedness. Jake was a part of her now. She could never hold anything back from him again.

"Maybe you don't want to feel anything, but I think you feel things so deeply that you can't let yourself acknowledge your feelings. I know, because I've been there. It's hell."

He slanted her a warning look, then scooped up the shirt his hands had eased from her such a short time before and held it out to her.

Their fingers touched, and he drew back as though even that casual joining hurt. He took three long strides away from her, putting the campfire between them before he stopped and took a deep ragged breath, his gaze going to the sky.

Hastily Regan pulled on her shirt and buttoned it with fingers that were suddenly awkward, her mind in a turmoil. Had she done something wrong? Pushed him too hard? Demanded too much? What?

"Are you sorry we made love?" she asked when she was covered again.

"I'll never be sorry about that, Regan." His voice roughened. "Never."

"Then why are you acting as though . . . as though you can't stand to touch me?"

"I don't love you. I can't let you think I do."

Regan realized she was holding her breath, and she let it out slowly. In the silence it sounded as loud as a sigh.

"I know that. Sometimes I think you barely like me."

"Then why the hell did you let me make love to you?" he asked harshly, then looked startled, as though that wasn't what he'd intended to say.

Regan nearly laughed with relief. So that was what was putting the tension in him. He was afraid of strings.

"I told you why. Tonight I needed you, and I think you needed me. Besides, I do love you, even though intellectually and almost every other way I know I shouldn't." She shrugged and met his gaze head on. "I just can't seem to help it. Once I make up my mind, I never change it."

"This time you'd be wise to make an exception," he said, his voice savage with some private emotion. "You can't possibly love me. You don't even know me." Turning his back, he bent to feed the fire until it blazed with angry fury between them.

"I know you better than you think I do, Jake."

"You know a fire fighter, a guy you see as a hero because that's what you need to see." He stood and slowly turned to face her. "I'm no hero."

"Of course you are! Look around you. It's men like you who save all this, men who risk their lives—"

"I'm not a fire fighter. I'm a prisoner at Donovan State Penitentiary in San Diego."

Eight

The words hung between them.

Regan felt her face go hot, then cold. She felt as though she was immersed in ice water. This was a joke, she told herself. A sick joke Jake was playing on her to keep her from getting too close. Wasn't it?

"I saw your coat. It had U.S. Forest Service stenciled on it," she said, measuring her words carefully. "And you said you'd been cutting a firebreak. Your hands—"

"The governor asked for inmate volunteers whose parole dates were already set. I was one of them."

Regan knew that prisoners were often used to fight fires during the height of California's summer fire season. That much she had to accept.

"But you're not a criminal. You can't be." She made a small helpless gesture with her hand.

The sound he made was too harsh to be called a laugh. "Funny, that's what I said every morning for three years when I woke up and saw the bars of my cell."

His cell.

Her surroundings blurred. The silence seemed to close in on her until she wanted to scream and scream and scream.

"Why...why did you tell me this now?"

Cutter watched her gaze slide away from him. He saw the subtle changes in her face, in her body. She was closing herself off from him inch by inch.

His eyes began to sting. From the smoke in the air, he told himself, but he knew he was only kidding himself.

"What's the difference? I told you. Let's leave it at that."

Acutely aware of him, even more acutely aware of the dull ache in her body put there by his lovemaking, she found her shorts and pulled them on.

From the age of sixteen, when her boyish shape had suddenly bloomed into the kind of figure her brothers had called jailbait, her mother had warned and warned her to be more wary of strangers, especially men. But she'd blithely gone about her slapdash life, trusting her instincts more than her intellect.

She'd been wrong about Tony.

Had she been wrong about Jake? Dangerously wrong?

Years of nightly news reports of women raped, women brutalized, women killed, shifted through her mind. Her thoughts darted wildly. To the miles of treacherous country between here and the nearest town, country he knew and she didn't. To the strength in his big hands and the cold glint that had been in his eyes when he'd nearly taken her head off for waking him. To the soul-shattering tenderness of his loving.

"We...should eat," she said, tying the tails of her shirt tightly around her waist. Was she armoring herself? she wondered with a vague flutter of amusement. Or trying to keep her feelings locked up inside? At the moment, she couldn't seem to make up her mind.

Without waiting for an answer she moved past him to the table she had laid out so meticulously. She picked up a sandwich, then put it down again.

"The bread's dried out," she said through lips that felt icy. "It'll probably taste like cardboard."

Suddenly she whirled, her hands twisting together against her stomach. "What happened, Jake?" she cried in an agonized whisper. "Why did they put you in prison?"

Cutter had expected the question. He hadn't expected the hard sickening thud in his gut when it came.

"Does it matter?" Don't ask me, he commanded silently. Don't make me tell you.

"Of course it matters! You can't make love to me one minute, then suddenly dump something like this on me the next."

He flinched. "I warned you. I told you to walk away."

Regan ignored the raw texture of his deep voice. "Tell me, Jake. You owe me that at least."

He went cold inside. He began to feel sick, as sick as he'd felt walking past row after row of cells, knowing that one of them would be his for a long long time.

Buying some time, he turned and walked to the edge of the circle of light. How could he say the words? How could he make her understand what no one else had understood? How, dear God, could he face the look in her eyes if she didn't?

He turned slowly, making himself face her. He cleared the thickness from his throat. Get it over with, man. She'll either understand or she won't.

"Before I went to prison, I was a cop, a detective sergeant working the kiddie detail. Missing kids. Molestation, that kind of stuff." He raised one eyebrow, and she nodded to indicate that she understood. She knew that he was weighing his words, worried about the effect they would have on her. She wanted to go to him, to smooth the tortured lines from his face and tell him that she understood. But she didn't. Dear God, how could she?

"One day I got this call from a woman, a mother who was afraid her four-year-old daughter, a little doll named Marissa, was being molested by the man who ran one of the biggest day-care centers in the city. His name was Greaves. Anton Greaves.''

Regan frowned. Had she read something about the man? The name was familiar. ''Why do I know that name?''

''He was a big shot in the governor's commission on education a few years back.''

''A former teacher?''

''Yeah, fourth grade.''

Suddenly her legs felt too weak to support her weight. Shaking uncontrollably, she walked to the nearest large rock and sat down.

''What . . . what did you do?''

''I ran a quick check and found the guy had impeccable credentials, a list of references as thick as a damn phone book. I would have felt comfortable entrusting Carole Ann to him, his record was that impressive.''

Falling silent, he arched his neck and tried to rub out the knot that had suddenly formed. Nothing could be harder than this. Nothing in the span of life left to him.

He bit off a sigh and made himself say the words that he'd tried so hard to keep inside, the words that had condemned him to hell.

''But the more I talked to him, the more my gut told me he was lying to me. The mother was divorced before the little girl was born. She worked two jobs, didn't have a boyfriend. The neighbors verified there were no men in her life.''

Regan wondered how he could sound so detached, and then realized he had unconsciously slipped into the persona of a cop. It was like a shield, protecting him, enabling him to function in the sewer of the streets. Or it had, she corrected herself grimly. Jake was no longer a cop. He was a convict. Even the word made her shudder.

''Did you arrest him?'' she asked in a barely audible tone. ''That man Greaves, I mean?''

''Eventually. It took six months, interviewing every parent on his list for the past five years, painstakingly putting it all together. I did it strictly by the book, documenting everything—parent interviews, medical reports, psychologists' reports.''

With quick impatience he brushed strands of unruly hair from his forehead. It was a rare nervous gesture, one she'd never seen before from him.

"The DA, a guy named Crandall, thought the case was thin, especially since Greaves had gotten himself a hotshot attorney with a habit of chewing up prosecutors who hadn't done their homework. Crandall kept stalling, asking for more evidence.''

He stopped, remembering the raging frustration he'd felt.

Maybe that was when he'd begun to think with his gut instead of his head. The same frustration clawed at him now. No matter how he told it, the story still had the same ending.

Unable to sit still any longer, Cutter walked to the limit of the fire's glow and stared at the open space around him. In his mind he heard angry voices, crude shouts, the shuddering clang of the bars sliding shut.

He turned and walked back to feed another log into the fire. Regan was sitting where he had left her, her arms folded across her waist, her eyes huge in her pale face.

Please don't look like that, he wanted to beg. Please don't hurt. Not because of me.

He took a deep breath and continued, "An informer I trusted told me Greaves had plans to leave the state, so I leaned on the DA.''

"Leaned on him how?''

"Everyone has a skeleton or two he wants to keep buried. I knew about one of his.''

Regan felt a chill pass over her. Cutter would be ruthless when he wanted something.

"I imagine the DA wasn't happy.''

Cutter snorted. "You imagine right. He tried the case like Greaves was made of glass. The case hinged on the video of Marissa talking to the kiddie shrink. Greaves's attorney claimed I coached her." His hand kneaded his neck, then returned to his side. "The guy was good, I'll give him that. By the time he finished, even I had my doubts."

Why can't I feel anything? she wondered. Shouldn't I be feeling something? Anything but this terrible numbness.

"What happened?" she managed to ask.

"The bastard walked."

She nearly cried out at the sudden flash of fury in his eyes. It was gone as quickly as it had come, but the memory lingered. This was not a man a rational person would deliberately make angry.

Regan shivered. "Surely the state jerked his day-care license?"

"The hell they did." His eyes chilled until they were pale with disgust. "The guy even had the nerve to sue the department for false arrest. Claimed I was out to make lieutenant and tried to frame him to do it. The shrinks told me he wouldn't stop. It was just a matter of catching him. So, whenever I was off duty, I shadowed him. One day I followed him to Brown Field. He was going to Mexico, he told me. To the interior." His voice took on a harsh tone. "Through the goodness of his heart, he'd volunteered to found an orphanage there."

Regan's hand flew to her mouth, but not before her anguished cry sliced between them.

Lost in his thoughts, Cutter didn't hear her. Telling Regan, somehow knowing that she knew exactly the kind of hell he'd gone through when Greaves had walked, feeling her reach out to him, had somehow made everything real to him again.

Sickeningly real.

In his mind he could see Greaves's oily smile flash as he spelled out the things he intended to do to the children entrusted to his care. Twisted, sick, evil things. Things that had made even a world-weary cynical cop like him cringe inside.

"Think of me tonight when you put your sweet little girl to bed," Greaves had said before he'd turned away to climb into the chartered Cessna standing at the far end of one of the runways.

Cutter remembered the rage that had filled him. And the savage feeling of helplessness.

Eighteen years of swallowing his pain, of fighting apathy and frustration and public scorn, of fighting a battle that no one could win, had exploded in one anguished terrible moment.

"I hit him," he said tonelessly. "When he fell, his head slammed against the wheel of the plane. The impact snapped his neck." He was speaking faster now, trying to get the words out before they choked him. "The pilot was in the control tower and saw the whole thing. I was charged with voluntary manslaughter. The prosecutor had a string of witnesses claiming I swore to bring Greaves down—one way or another. The jury found me guilty. The judge gave me eight years. I've served three. I was due for parole in eleven months."

Cutter lifted his right hand and looked at it. Slowly, inexorably, his fingers clenched into a powerful fist. When he spoke again, his voice was raw with savage twisting emotion.

"I was a good cop, Regan. I cut my share of corners, yes, but I swear to you, I *never* intended to kill him."

The fire popped, spattering the stones with sizzling embers. Standing as still as the air, Cutter watched the firelight flicker against the darkness. He tried to make himself numb inside. This time it didn't work.

Making love to Regan had blasted him open, exposing the feelings he'd buried so deep for so long. His emotions were alive and twisting, clawing at him. There were all kinds of prisons. Feelings were the worst of all.

Next to him, he felt Regan move. He sensed her gaze on his face and turned slowly to look at her. His eyes were bleak, his mouth white. "Do you believe me?"

She thought about the stillness in his eyes and knew he could kill. But deliberately? In cold blood, the way the jury had believed?

In her mind echoed something she'd read, something from Nietzsche: "Whoever fights monsters should see to it that in the process he does not become a monster."

Cutter felt as though he were strangling. He couldn't seem to get enough air in his lungs. "Is that what you think I am? A monster?"

The low throb of pain in his voice was like a stab in her heart, and Regan realized she'd spoken the words aloud.

She felt the tension radiating from his big body. His face was still, his eyes slitted. It was the look of a man who was in agony, in his body, in his soul. His need was a living thing, reaching out to her, touching her in a place she had never allowed any man to go before.

Without hesitating, her expression as open as his was guarded, she reached up to touch the lines etched between his brows.

"No, my darling. I think you cared too much and made a very human, very tragic mistake. I'm just so sorry you had to suffer for it."

Her fingers traced the mouth she'd felt soften against her lips. On an indrawn breath that sounded tortured, he caught her hand and brushed a hard kiss into the palm before trapping her fingers in his hard grip.

"No one. No one believed me. Not even my wife."

"Oh, Jake," she whispered in a trembling voice. "No wonder you're so hurt inside."

He pulled her hard against his chest. His kiss was hungry, the kind that came from years and years of wanting. Regan met his need eagerly, without reservation.

His fingers wound into her soft hair, releasing the delicate scent of her shampoo. He kissed her until she was breathless, then slid his mouth down the smooth line of her throat to touch his tongue to the frantic pulse beating there.

His mouth was warm, seeking, sliding to the tender spot beneath her ear. She shivered, and he raised his head.

"I don't want to hurt you, Regan. Not ever. All I can give you is tonight."

Regan heard the ring of truth in his deep tortured voice. She also heard the warning. If she didn't walk away from him now, whatever happened would be on her head. If she got hurt...

She left the thought unfinished. Now wasn't a time for doubts. Nor was it a time for thought. Now was a time for feeling.

"After Tony left me, I felt...bruised inside. I told myself I was still a desirable woman even though I couldn't have children, but..."

She shrugged self-consciously. "From the first moment I saw you, I started feeling alive again. You're not like any man I've ever met. Mostly you make me uncomfortable, because you're blunt and hard-edged and...dangerous. But when you kissed me that first time, you made me feel beautiful and sexy and...and whole. That's what you can give me tonight."

His fingers moved her head to just the right angle to meet his mouth. "You *are* beautiful, Regan." His voice throbbed with deep rich feeling. "Inside, outside, every way that counts."

"So are you."

She decided that the softened corners of his mouth constituted a smile and congratulated herself. Tonight she would keep the shadows out of his eyes. Tonight she would make him forget the horrors that had put those shadows there.

"Isn't the night wonderful?" She slid her arms around his neck and brought her body close to his. "The air is so soft. Do you smell the pines?"

Without waiting for an answer, she nuzzled his strong neck. He was still very tense. She caressed his muscles, her fingers trying to ease the knots she felt there.

Shadows surrounded them, turning the day into a soft silent twilight. The fire cast a circle of light around them. Somewhere in the distance an owl hooted. The breeze blew like a benediction through the pine needles.

"Listen," she said, cocking her head. "Can you hear the music in the wind?"

Cutter saw the innocence in her eyes and the smile that trembled on her mouth. He saw a dream. "You're my music." This time his smile came more easily, and Regan wanted to shout.

"Dance with me, Jake. Please."

He pressed her head into the hollow of his shoulder and pulled her close. Whatever she wanted, he would try to give her. He would hold off tomorrow for as long as he could. For both of them.

"It's been a long time since I've danced," he said with a trace of self-consciousness. "I was never much good even then. Don't expect too much."

"It's been a long time for me, too." She clung to him, listening to the rapid beat of his heart beneath her cheek. His thighs were hard against hers, moving with a rhythm that came from the heat in his blood.

Regan moved with him, enveloped in his strong powerful arms, warmed by the heat of his tense body. The pebbled ground beneath them created a delicious friction under her feet.

She lost track of time. Or did it stand still for them?

Nothing mattered but the tantalizing heat Jake was creating in her, a heat that was pure sensation, pure bliss. Little shivers like warm rippling waves spread through her, filling every part of her until she felt soft and ready inside. Finally the heat seemed unbearable. Arching against him, she tried to rub away the ache.

He stopped moving. Beneath her cheek, his heart changed tempo, faltering, then doubling its frantic rhythm. His arms tightened.

"Stand still," he whispered. "Give me a minute. I'm out of practice."

Slowly he eased away from her, his head down, his eyes closed. His breathing rasped painfully between them.

She drew her hands from his neck, letting them rest on his shoulders, aware of the ripple of muscle beneath his warm skin. Loving the feel of him, intoxicated by the musky scent of his skin, she let her hands move lower, luxuriating in the rough texture of his skin where the fine golden hair covered it.

He stepped back, breathing hard, his eyes glittering. She stopped, confused. As their eyes met, he lifted his eyebrows and extended his arms slightly, as if to say he was all hers.

A laugh bubbled in her throat. "That looks like a challenge to me, Cutter."

"You gonna take me up on it?" His slow sensuous smile was a gift, holding her, thrilling her.

"Absolutely. We'll see who breaks first."

Slowly, letting herself savor the way his muscles flexed under her touch, she slid his shirt off him. It fell to the ground behind him, covering part of the blanket she'd flung aside in her haste to go to him.

With a soft sigh, she leaned forward to kiss his shoulder, sliding her lips back and forth over his warm flesh. His muscles contracted on a quick indrawn breath, and she drew back to replace her mouth with her hands.

Eagerly, lovingly, they moved down his hard chest, her palms warming from the friction of the soft hair against her skin. His belly was flat, corded, warm, arrowed in the middle by hair that flared over his belly button.

Regan hesitated, then slid the metal tab of his zipper downward. Her fingers slid against heated male flesh, reminding her that he'd pulled his jeans on over bare skin.

Cutter released a shuddering groan that seemed wrung from deep inside. His mouth found hers again. This time his tongue plunged deep, wringing a moan of pleasure from her that seemed to inflame him even more.

With an awkward haste that told her more than any words could how much he wanted her, his hands tore at the knot of her shirttails. When they were hanging free, he ripped open the buttons of her shirt and slid it from her shoulders.

In the fading light her skin was like cream, smooth, rich, and so enticing that Cutter had trouble breathing. Her breasts were full and firm. Even though the blood pounding through his rigid flesh urged him to hurry, he made himself take time to look at her. He would have to live on this memory for a long time.

In the hot glow from the fire, Regan saw something come into his eyes. It was too powerful, too compelling, to be labeled. She only knew it made her feel like soaring.

Slowly, reverently, he bent his head. The moist heat of his tongue on her nipple brought a shivering gasp from her. Her fingers moved in his hair, clenching, unclenching, with the nearly unbearable pleasure he was exciting in her. Her knees buckled, and she would have slid down his body if he hadn't caught her in his strong embrace.

"Please, Jake. I . . . hurt."

His arm encircled her shoulders, and he dragged her against him, his kiss exploding against her mouth. His arms moved lower, locking around her waist. He lifted her from her feet, his powerful arms holding her as though she weighed nothing. She wrapped her arms around his neck and met his fevered mouth eagerly before he took them to the rumpled blanket.

"Hurry," she whispered, tugging at the open waistband of his jeans.

His hands replaced hers, tugging the jeans over his legs until he was naked again.

And then he was bending over her, his fingers stroking, kneading, finding her ready. He lay next to her, then rolled until she was on top of him, her legs straddling his hips.

"Jake?" she whispered in an agony of need. Never had she been the one to find her own rhythm. Never had she been the one in control. The possibilities both exhilarated and terrified her.

As though he sensed her thoughts, Jake gentled her with callused hands on her soft thighs. "Easy," he whispered. "Take it slow, fast, any way you want."

With his hands and his hips, he helped her settle over him. She was slick and hot, taking the throbbing, aching length of his arousal into her so slowly that he had trouble keeping his groans inside.

He thought he'd known all there was to know about sexual need, but the moment she began to move, he knew that no other woman had ever touched him, really touched the man inside, the way Regan touched him. No other woman had ever made him want the way Regan made him want.

His muscles tensed, beginning to burn from the effort he was expending to let her control him. His fists clenched around handfuls of blanket. Sweat broke out on his skin.

She was above him, moving wildly, her breath coming in small eager gasps. Her face was flushed, and so beautiful it made him hurt to look at her. Years and years of loneliness and longing merged into a vision that was Regan.

He felt the last of his resistance burn into need. His teeth ground on a desperate aching moan. She moved faster, her skin dewy with the sweat of passion. He strained against the need to ease the hot clawing agony she'd aroused in him. He felt his blood pound, the heat drench him, the ache grind in him, until it was impossible to breathe.

And then she was calling his name in a rush of release, her fingers digging into his shoulders. With a harsh cry he reached for her and crushed her to him, his body pulsing into hers in hot waves.

She collapsed on top of him, her long lashes fluttering against his shoulder. He held her close, easing the small tremors that still shook her. She sighed, murmured something, then smiled again.

"What, honey?" he asked in a rough tone. He never wanted to let her go.

"I still hear beautiful, beautiful music."

Cutter did, too. The kind that made a man want to make promises and plan a future. He rubbed his chin against her soft hair and tried not to think about tomorrow. Or the day after that. Or the months he would spend trying to get this night out of his mind.

A feeling took hold in him, making him hurt the way he'd hurt when he heard the jury's verdict. Tonight, for the first time, he knew, really knew, what prison had taken from him.

Nine

Regan awoke slowly, not knowing at first what had made her open her eyes. Warm and cozy under the blanket, she stretched languidly, feeling delightfully relaxed.

"Open your eyes, honey." Jake was arched over her, braced on his elbows, his bare chest inches from her breasts, one of his legs angled over hers.

"Is it morning already?" she whispered, her voice sleepy.

"First light."

He bent to brush a kiss over her mouth. Eagerness quickened inside her. No matter how many times she felt his mouth on hers, she could never get over the wonder of it.

"You were smiling in your sleep. I hated to wake you." His breath bathed her face, exciting her senses.

"That's because I was dreaming about you."

"Were you?" His expression was controlled, but an emotion she didn't recognize seethed in his eyes. She wanted it to be love. She wouldn't let herself believe it was.

"Mmm. You were making love to me. I liked it." She brushed a stray lock of sandy hair from his forehead. He turned his head to burn a kiss into her wrist, making her pulse rocket. She started to reach for him, but he stopped her.

"Look to your right," he whispered. "By that clump of holly."

Regan turned onto her stomach, her questioning gaze following the direction of his glance. A fragile-looking doe and her fawn stood next to the bushes, drinking from the stream. The baby, his soft tan coat dappled with darker spots, was very young and still unsteady on his long wobbly legs.

"Oh," she whispered in delight, her hand reaching for Jake's. "Isn't he darling?"

"It's a buck," he teased. "Bucks aren't darling."

"This one is."

She and Jake lay side by side, his arm stretched across her shoulders. It was so quiet that she could hear the sound of the fawn's tongue lapping the water.

The mother stood by protectively, every few seconds raising her head to sniff the air and look around. Having drunk his fill, the baby nuzzled his mother's side, eager to nurse. The doe nudged him away, then bent to nibble grass.

"Teaching by example," Regan whispered, giving Jake a grin.

"Best way, or so they tell me."

But the fawn was having none of it. Instead, with the determination of a linebacker, he burrowed his head beneath his mother's belly, his mouth eager. With what looked like motherly resignation, the pretty little doe stood quietly, now and then nuzzling her baby's flank with her nose.

Emotion seized Regan's throat, and she was afraid to speak. The moment was so special, so beautiful. With a sensitivity that was more special than he knew, Jake had given it to her. She wanted more of these moments with him. A lifetime.

"Such a little love," she murmured in a thick voice. "And so stubborn."

A low rumbling noise intruded into the stillness. A tanker was flying along the ridge line, too high for them to make out the numbers on the fuselage. The orange wingtips were bright splotches of color in the gray dawn.

The doe's head came up, her ears rigid. Sensing his mother's tension, the fawn stopped nursing.

The engine noise bounced off the cliffs, reverberating like thunder through the clearing. With a scuffle of small hooves, mother and baby bolted into the pines, white tails raised.

"Be safe," Regan whispered, watching them until they disappeared.

Jake's arm pulled her close. "Why do I think you cry at old movies, too?"

"All my life people have been telling me I'm too emotional. I even fall apart over those commercials on TV, the ones that tell you to reach out and touch someone."

She turned her head and looked at him. Her eyes were still filled with the wonder of the moment they'd shared. Her smooth skin was still flushed from the warmth of sleep. Cutter had never seen a woman who was more beautiful or more desirable. He turned onto his back and raised a hand to caress her cheek.

"God, I wish things were different," he said in a raw tone. "But I can't change the things I've done. I can't make them go away as though they don't matter. Because they do."

She stroked his thick beard with trembling fingers. "I know that, and I understand. Last night was special, Jake. I'll never forget it. Thank you for giving it to me."

One side of his mouth moved in a crooked smile that ended far too quickly, as though it felt uncomfortable on those hard lips. "You gave me something special last night, too."

Her questioning look brought another quick half smile. "You believed in me. I'll live on that for a long time."

He ran his hand through his hair. It was clean and shiny, the color of summer grass. It tumbled over his bruised forehead without any kind of order.

Suddenly she saw him as he must have been as a cop, eager to make a difference, filled with ideals, without the shadows in his eyes, without the scars on his face and the bruises on his soul. He'd given so much, cared so deeply, fought so hard—only to end up so terribly alone.

Tenderness filled her. Jake needed her, no matter what he claimed. She touched the corner of his mouth. "I'll always believe in you, Jake, even when you can't believe in yourself."

He took her mouth over and over with light tender kisses that quickly fired the longing that she'd felt since the first time he kissed her.

She closed her eyes, giving in to the yearning filling her. As though he sensed her need, he deepened the kiss, his tongue sliding between her parted lips to taste her mouth at will.

The hunger of last night was gone, but this kiss was just as potent, just as stirring. Her skin began to warm where his beard rubbed. Her lips began to tremble. She gave herself up to the passion surging between them, her body eager to feel him inside her again.

"God, Regan," he whispered hoarsely against her mouth. "I feel like I'm drowning whenever I touch you." With a groan, he pulled away and hung his head, his breath rasping between them. "We can't do this," he managed to say in a reasonable tone. "The night is over."

Regan thought about the throbbing heat building inside her. She had never felt as good as she felt this morning. Suddenly she realized the closeness they'd shared had turned her into a greedy woman.

She wanted another night like last night, and then another. She wanted a long string of nights—and days—with Jake. Her smile felt soft and liquid as she brushed his tumbled hair from his forehead.

"Looks like night to me." Her voice was husky with the need she didn't bother to hide.

Cutter sat up and rested his arm on the knee drawn close to his broad chest. He looked away, toward the rugged slopes surrounding them. His profile was aggressively male, indomitably strong.

"Tonight. Tonight you'll be in a nice clean bed someplace safe, I promise."

"Stay there with me."

He inhaled with a ragged smile. "You know I can't."

She knew all too well. While she would be free to come and go, he would be back in a cell. Caged like an animal.

She sat up and rested her cheek against his warm shoulder. "I'll visit as often as I can, and when you're paroled, I'll be there," she promised, running her fingers down the corded length of the arm braced between them. His reaction was lightning quick, a visible shiver, a tightening of his jaw.

"Jake—"

He stopped her words with a hungry kiss that ended too soon. "Be quiet a minute, and listen to me." This time the command in his voice was softened by a weariness that told her he intended to say something she wasn't going to like.

Tony had sounded like that just before he'd told her about his young mistress.

"No," she said sharply, trying to pull out of his arms. "Whatever it is, I don't want to hear it."

"You have to." His hand circled her wrist, holding her immobile as though she were nothing more than a reed. "Please, Regan. Don't make this harder than it already is."

The tortured note in his voice calmed her.

"I'm listening."

She would always listen, Cutter thought with an inner sigh. And she would always be there for the man who owned her heart. He wondered if she knew how much he coveted the love she was offering so freely. He wondered if she could understand how deeply it hurt him that he couldn't return it.

He loosened his hand, his fingers still pressed to her frantic pulse. Seeing that she wasn't going to run from him, he let her go.

"While we were cutting that firebreak on the ridge, something happened. The details aren't important. The bottom line is, I hit a guard. That means no parole for sure. Extra time served, probably in a maximum-security prison. Folsom, maybe, or San Quentin. Even if they could find room for me in the special sections for ex-cops, I wouldn't survive it. The guards take care of their own."

Regan gasped. "Oh, no, Jake. No!" She clutched his hand, her eyes riveted to his. She was so upset that she didn't see the stark look of pain cross his face.

"Philip is a defense attorney, one of the best in the country. I'll talk to him." She had an irrational urge to talk louder, as though that could keep the fear generated by his blunt words at bay. "There has to be something we can do. Philip will know. As soon as we reach a phone, I'll call him. He'll help you, I know he will."

"No, he won't, Regan. I asked him to defend me. He turned me down flat."

"Then...then we'll find someone else. They can't just put you someplace where... where you don't have a chance."

Cutter looked into her eyes. The sleepy look of satisfaction he'd put there was gone. Instead she looked bruised. Lost.

A feeling he couldn't define sifted past his defenses. He wanted to remember her jerking her chin at him and giving him hell. He wanted to remember her flushed and eager for his kiss. He knew that instead he would remember the pain he'd caused her.

"You know better than that," he told her. "Life doesn't work that way. Once I thought it did, a lifetime ago. Now I know it doesn't." He glanced toward the south. "I'm not going back."

"Not . . . you mean you're escaping?"

"I'm as good as dead, anyway."

"But...but sooner or later they'll catch you and make you go back."

His face tightened. "I'll never go back. *Never*. Nothing is as important as freedom, not even my life."

Regan felt an icy hand clutch her throat. Jake was going to die. It might be soon, or it might not happen for months or even years, but sooner or later he would die, his magnificent body riddled with bullets.

The blood drained from her face. Her lips felt numb as she schooled her features into masklike blankness. "Where will you go?"

Cutter watched her eyes. She was too calm, too accepting. He'd seen that frozen look too many times not to recognize shock when he saw it.

He swore under his breath before answering calmly, "A guy who did time in Donovan lives in Tijuana. He arranges jobs for guys like me."

A suffocating need to move overtook him, almost as though he were still in his cell. He got to his feet and pulled on his jeans. He found his socks and boots in the jumble of packs and blankets littering the campsite and sat down on a log to pull them on.

Regan emerged from the blanket, which felt cold without his warmth, and pulled on her shirt. She was on her feet before she knew it, moving over to him, reaching out to touch his rigid back.

"Don't push me away, Jake. I love you."

He flinched. "Stress does funny things to people. Makes them act irrationally, emotionally. When you think you're going to die, you can convince yourself of anything. When you're safely back in your nice sane world, you'll realize that."

"You think I'm like your ex-wife, but I'm not."

Cutter jerked the bootlace into a knot, then hunkered down to poke the embers into life before adding the last of the kindling. When the flames licked hot, he added a length of pine and watched it catch.

Numbly she found her sneakers and a clean pair of socks.

"What kind of a job?" she asked, as though everything were settled. But it wasn't, not for her. She wasn't going to let Cutter leave her, not without a fight.

"Turk brokers men. Mercenaries."

Regan took a precisely measured breath. Everything inside her was screaming a denial. "You're going to kill for money?"

His head whipped toward her. His eyes were alive with a seething emotion that was as strong as rage, but subtly different.

"Don't try to lay that trip on me, Regan," he said in a low tone. "I was a soldier before I was a cop. I got paid to kill then, and no one complained. I exchanged one uniform for another, that's all. I can do it again."

"That's not true, and you know it. You'd hate it, every minute of it. A man like you has to believe in what he's fighting for."

"Oh, I believed all right," he said with a bottomless weariness. Without knowing he was doing it, he rubbed the place where the handcuffs had dug into his wrists. "And I cared, cared so much I used to have nightmares about the people I couldn't help. For all the good it did me. Now it's time I started caring about myself."

The absolute certainty that he was making a terrible mistake made Regan forget her resolve to go carefully. She got to her feet and went to him, the fire searing her bare legs as she passed.

"Turning yourself into a killing machine isn't caring, Jake. Sooner or later you'll hate yourself because you know what you're doing is wrong, and that'll scar you worse than any prison."

He stood up so fast that she stepped back in alarm. He reached for her, his hands closing around her arms in a powerful angry grip.

"Don't talk to me about prison," he commanded, giving her a shake. "You can't begin to imagine what it's like, living like an animal, fighting every day to stay alive, the mind games you play to keep from giving up."

He held her chin and made her look at him. "Prison changes a man, Regan. Inside, where it doesn't show. It makes him hard and cynical and sometimes vicious."

"You're not vicious!" she cried. "Not you."

"You're wrong. Everyone in prison learns to be vicious in order to survive. Otherwise, he ends up dead or a whore."

Regan flinched. "You're not either of those."

"No, but I'm not the kind of man who can let himself love you, although, God knows, I wish I could be."

Joy ripped through her heart. "But you are, Jake!" she exclaimed eagerly. "Don't go to Mexico. Please. Stay here with me. Let me help you, be with you. Philip knows people in Sacramento. Nothing is impossible unless you believe it is."

His face twisted, and he drew in a violent lungful of air. "Prison is just one big garbage pail, Regan. I tried to keep my head above water, but sooner or later, I would have ended up just like the other pieces of human garbage. Anything is better than that. *Anything*."

He pushed her away from him so savagely that she stumbled. His face twisted, but he didn't apologize. "I'm going to scout around for the best way out of here. Be ready to leave when I get back."

The birds had stopped singing. Or had they sensed the approach of the flames and flown to safety? Regan couldn't seem to make herself care.

Jittery and tense, she stood next to a giant Douglas fir, her fingers picking at the scaly bark. Even though the day had only just started, the air was warm and heavy—almost as heavy as the lump in her stomach.

Jake had been gone for an hour. She'd eaten a piece of dry bread, drunk burned coffee, repacked the satchels. After that, she'd paced until she'd begun to get a headache. It was still pounding in her temple.

One more day, she thought. That was all they had. A few hours. After that she would never see him again. The man she loved. The man who had made her feel whole again.

The man who was also an escaped convict.

It couldn't be true, it *shouldn't* be true, but it was.

No matter how many times she took his words and tried to reshape them, they always ended up the same way. Jake was going to spend the rest of his life on the run, risking his life for anyone with the money to pay.

The very thought made her sick inside.

She'd always heard that mercenaries were desperate ruthless men, men without conscience. Jake was desperate, yes, and the hard look in his eyes when she'd first seen him had told her that he could be ruthless. But he wasn't without conscience. A man without conscience would have left her to fend for herself at the cabin. A man without conscience would have taken her quickly, savagely, without tenderness, without caring. A man without conscience wouldn't have told her the truth about himself, believing even as he did that she would turn away from him the way others had before.

But Jake had risked his own safety for her. And he had restrained his own needs, three long punishing empty years of need, in order to bring her satisfaction first.

A rustle in the tallest pine drew her gaze. With a controlled flurry of feathered muscle and sinew, a hawk winged upward, independent and proud and unafraid. Such a magnificent creature would ultimately die in captivity, she knew, but not before he'd done all he could to escape.

Regan stared blindly at the sky.

Dear God, how had Jake stood it? she wondered. It must have been indescribable agony, living day after day in physical and emotional confinement. No wonder he was cynical and bitter. No wonder he no longer believed in anything but himself.

She shuddered. Oh, Jake, she cried silently. I don't want you to leave.

She slumped back against the tree and closed her eyes. If only they'd met at a different place, at a different time. If only they'd had more days and nights together. If only...if only too many things.

"I'm sorry."

How had Jake managed to get so close without her hearing him? she wondered, as she opened her eyes and saw him standing a few yards from the stream.

She managed a smile. She wasn't going to spoil these last few hours. "I'm sorry, too. I warned you, I'm too emotional." Her voice wobbled, but she kept her chin up and her smile in place. She *would not* cry. Because if she started, if she gave in to the violent emotions inside her, she just might crack wide open.

He stood perfectly still, his shoulders angled in the proud line she would always remember. "Wrong. You're perfect. Someone needs to tell you that often enough so that you finally believe it."

"You could, if I went with you."

"No, Regan."

He looked so right in this place, with his wind-tangled hair and rough-hewn features. His long restless legs needed this kind of space. His fierce spirit needed this kind of savage beauty for nourishment. Like a hawk.

A wave of love and longing traveled down her body. How many months would it take before she stopped remembering the feel of his hands on her skin? How many years before she stopped missing the rare magic of his husky laughter?

"I really do love you, Jake. I think I always will."

He turned away, but not before she'd seen the spasm cross his face. The simple motion was more eloquent than any words, and Jake would never be a man who used words easily.

"We'd better go." He sounded incredibly weary.

"Not yet. I want you to make love to me again."

That caught him by surprise. He turned quickly to stare at her as though she'd plowed a fist into his flesh. For a moment she thought he was going to sweep her into his powerful arms and crush her, so fierce was the look that came into his eyes. To her acute disappointment, however, when he spoke his voice revealed nothing but barely restrained impatience.

"We have a long day ahead of us. I've risked your safety enough as it is."

"Or I'll make love to you," she continued, as though he hadn't spoken.

"No." This time his voice was steel.

Regan moved closer, her skin beginning to warm at the thought of his hands caressing her. She'd never seduced a man before. She'd never wanted to. But in her own way, she was as desperate as Jake. Desperate to have one more taste of that hard mouth that had softened just for her, desperate to feel the potent thrust of his body making them one, desperate for one more memory to take with her when he walked away.

"Why not?" Her words were as soft as a sigh, but laced with a stubborn determination her friends and family had learned to respect.

"Dammit, Regan," Cutter began, then stopped, suddenly forgetting what he had to say.

With the same stubbornness in her eyes, she crossed her arms over her body to strip her T-shirt over her head, revealing her lush breasts. Her skin glowed with an inner sunshine, making his breath catch.

When he'd left her, he had walked at top speed toward the ridge, hoping to exhaust his body and dull his mind so that he wouldn't think about the woman he was leaving behind. He'd thought he'd succeeded. Now he knew that he'd only been kidding himself.

She had only to smile in that crooked irresistibly sexy way and he was hooked all over again. As he watched, she pulled the band from her thick ponytail and began threading her fingers through the gold-streaked silk until it framed her face with rich brown color.

The thought of her slender warm fingers stroking him in that same slow way sent a shaft of hot longing stabbing through him. He closed his eyes, fighting the need that threatened to send him to his knees as nothing else had ever done.

"Regan, the damn fire's only a few hours away from here." His voice had a strangled quality that brought a honeyed curve to her lips.

"Come inside me, Jake," she murmured, her hands sliding her shorts from her long sleekly curving thighs, letting them fall to the ground. She stepped free. "Be with me one more time."

"No." He took in her tousled hair, her glowing eyes, her mouth reddened and swollen from the night's passion. A lifetime of need was compressed into this one moment, making him bleed inside. God, how he needed this crazy, impossible, breathtaking woman.

"Please, Jake."

Cutter took a slow breath, trying to withstand the heated pressure between his legs, need making him so hot and rigid that he groaned out her name before he could stop himself.

Without answering, she walked into his arms, offering her mouth. Need overpowering his will to resist, he took what she offered, his kiss hungry, hot, possessive.

He pulled his mouth from hers and began raining kisses on her face, her neck, her lips again. He murmured her name between kisses, and she met him with lips just as hot, a need just as great, so great she was awash in sensation, drowning in wild shivering desire.

His powerful muscles bulged like coiled steel, trying to pull her closer. She strained, too, trying to imprint every inch of him on her body.

His hands roamed her skin, his rough fingers rubbing her breasts until they were heavy and aching for his mouth. His tongue moistened the tips, intensely provocative, achingly hungry.

It had never been like this for her before. Need built like wildfire, until she couldn't stand it. Wedging her hands between them, she frantically tugged at his shirt, drawing it free. Sensing her need, he quickly unsnapped his jeans, worked the zipper.

"Hurry," she whispered, her hands busy on his shirt buttons.

"Not a chance, honey. This has to last me a long time." His voice was graveled and raw with hunger. Pushing aside her hands, he rid himself of his clothes quickly, efficiently, knowing that she was watching impatiently, eagerly, even as she was slipping out of her panties and shedding those ridiculous pink sneakers.

"Come with me," he said when she reached for him again, her slender body ripe and yearning. He took her hand and led her to the rich thick blanket of emerald grass by the stream.

Together they sank to their knees on the cool carpet. Then Cutter's hands eased her to her back, and she sighed at the coolness of the coarse blades pressing against her bare skin. The scent of pine was strong. The song of the stream was hypnotic and slow.

Cutter watched her eyes search his as her hands reached for him, drawing him closer. She touched him, stroked him until he felt a need for her that bordered on desperate.

The words to tell her what she had come to mean to him were in his heart, but the self-protective habit of a lifetime kept him from sharing them. He was too wounded, too scarred, too bitter, to let anyone have that kind of power over him ever again.

Still, he longed for her in a way that made him hurt inside. Gentleness had never come easy for him, but he tried. His hand covered hers, drawing it slowly to his mouth. He kissed her wrist where her pulse throbbed visibly beneath the delicate skin, brushed his mouth across her palm.

Regan shivered at the exquisite slide of his whiskers over her skin. She writhed, arching upward, inviting him to fill her.

Ignoring the need scalding him, he made himself go slowly, stroking her until she quivered under his hands, kissing her until she moaned helplessly.

Regan felt his restraint, his tenderness. It was in the gentle slide of his hard fingers over the hot moist mound that quivered to feel his penetration. It was in the soft brush of his kiss over her rigid aching nipples.

She clung to him, riding on a wave of love and need. Cutter felt his control slipping. Her soft whimpers told him she was ready. He himself was close to bursting.

Using his knee, he nudged her thighs wider, tested her readiness, found her hot and moist, then settled into her until he was fully sheathed, their bodies all but fused.

They moved together, found the timeless rhythm of intimacy that made two people one mind, one soul. Cutter tried to keep the small piece of himself safe, the part of him no one saw, no one knew. But with each movement, each wildly responsive moan he wrung from her, he found himself giving her all that he was, all that he had. For the first and only time in his life, all his barriers were down. He was hers, only hers.

Regan clutched his shoulders, lost in the pleasure suffusing her heated body. As soon as she'd taken him inside, his tenderness had turned into a driving need that seemed to consume him. His steely control was gone. He took her with a wild need that bordered on violent. Her own need was just as elemental, just as primitive, in its savage demand. She writhed against him, begging with her mouth and hands for more.

His kiss crushed her mouth. Her body quivering, straining, pulsing, she hung on to him, knowing only him, wanting only his potency filling her, feeling the hot ecstasy of release convulsing her.

He exploded into her, his body shuddering with hard tremors, his breath coming out in a tortured cry against her breast.

Then he collapsed against her, his weight crushing her into the thick grass. His chest heaved; his breathing was ragged and hoarse. His skin was drenched in sweat.

Regan cradled him willingly, her own breath settling slowly. Gently, lovingly, she smoothed her fingers down his long back, feeling the powerful muscles ripple, then relax, under her touch.

Her heart filled with love. He was vulnerable to her now, for however long he allowed her to hold him like this. With fingers that weren't quite steady, she brushed the ragged strands of unruly hair from his damp forehead, exposing the tape she'd put there.

Would he find someone in Mexico to love him? she wondered. To bind his wounds and kiss away the shadows in his eyes?

Her eyes closed on a terrible sadness, her lashes pressed tightly together against the hot rush of tears. She wanted to beg him to forget about escaping, to finish his sentence, to come to her when he was finally freed. To let her love heal him. To make him smile again.

But how could she ask the man she loved to endure years of degradation and emotional torture for her? How could she ask him to risk his life?

She couldn't, and it was killing her.

Her arms tightened. As though she'd wakened him, he sighed heavily and rolled away from her. He sat up, hooked one arm over his raised knee and looked immediately toward the ridge. The smoke was thicker.

"I know. We have to go," she said, smiling up at him. He turned to look down at her.

His answering smile ended on a muttered curse. She caught his hand before it could close into a fist and held it against her cheek.

"It's all right, Jake. I won't make a scene, I promise."

A look she'd never seen before crossed his face, a look that made her hold her breath. "Regan, I want you to promise me that you won't worry about me. I can handle this if I know you'll put it behind you and go on with your life."

She kissed his wrist. The slight puckering of the skin caught her eye. Another scar. From steel handcuffs worn too tightly for too many hours.

She forced a smile as she met his gaze. "I promise I won't worry. But I can't promise I won't miss you. Maybe I'll even grieve a little, probably go through a gross of peanut-butter miniatures, but I'll be fine."

His pupils dilated, his wolf-proud eyes impaling her. Why had she ever thought those beautiful eyes were cold? she wondered, touching the corner of his hard mouth with her finger.

"Now you do something for me," she whispered.

"What?"

"Smile for me."

He looked uncomfortable, even as his mouth slanted crookedly into a quick self-conscious smile. Before she could imprint his rough beautiful face onto her memory, he bent to brush his mouth against hers.

"Time to go," he said, pulling her to her feet.

They dressed quickly in silence. The trickling of the stream and the slide of clothing against skin were the only sounds in the glade.

Before they set off, Regan offered Cutter the last of their bread and coffee. He gulped the coffee from the pan in three swallows, but refused the bread after a quick glance over his shoulder at the growing darkness over the ridge.

"Save it," he ordered as he shouldered both their packs. "We'll need to rest in a couple of hours. I'll eat then."

When she was safely along the path, he turned to look back. The trees on the ridge had caught fire. In a few hours, maybe less, all that would be left of the place where they had made love was blackened ash.

Ten

Several hours later, Cutter found the trail intersecting with the abandoned logging road angling down into Tatum's Bend, the closest of the foothill towns.

The narrow track was winding and steep, the hard dirt overlaid with oak leaves and pine needles, making footing treacherous. High-altitude vegetation gave way to deciduous trees and live oaks. The underbrush was thicker, overhanging the trail in spots, making passage difficult.

By the time the slope eased into flat ground and open space, Regan's bare legs were crisscrossed with angry red scratches, and her shirt was torn in several places, where low-lying branches had caught her by surprise. She was out of breath and exhausted, her throat raw. She craved rest.

Just when she knew she couldn't take one more step, Jake called a halt. With a thankful groan, she sank onto the nearest rock and hung her head between her knees.

Smoke was everywhere, limiting visibility and stinging her nostrils. The air was alive with ash.

"Definitely should have gone to the beach," she muttered between heaving breaths. Her ears were ringing, her eyes watering. She tried to take small breaths, but even those burned. She tried to swallow, tasted grit. A spasm of coughing shook her.

"We're in trouble, aren't we?" she asked as she handed him the bottle and watched him drink.

"We'll make it. Just don't get too comfortable. We can't stop long."

Cutter looked around quickly, then eased the pack from his shoulder and settled on the ground next to her. He was worried. Even though he couldn't see through the haze, he could hear the sound of tankers overhead. The wind had shifted, blowing directly toward them.

They needed to keep moving, but Regan needed rest. He hated to admit it, but he did, too.

"How much farther?" Regan asked.

"No more than six miles. The road should be just beyond that ravine. After that, it's an easy walk to town."

One she would take by herself, she thought sadly. She would think of him with each step she took.

Cutter dug into her bag and pulled out the last of their food. She was too tired to eat, but when he offered her a piece of bread, she took it because she knew he would insist.

"What about you?" she asked when she had swallowed the last dry crumb. "The interstate is between you and the border. How will you get across?"

"At night."

At night like the *coyotes* who brought Mexican nationals into the country illegally. The sudden lump in her throat made it hard to swallow.

"I have almost a hundred dollars with me," she said in a deliberately casual tone. "I want you to take it."

"No."

Cutter heard the drone of airplane engines and searched the sky, but the smoke was too thick for him to see anything above the treetops.

"Jake, please."

"Dammit, *no!* I don't want your money."

"But—"

"Regan, stop talking for once. Rest."

She remembered her promise to keep up with him. Was he remembering, too? Was that all he would remember, a woman who irritated him and challenged him and gave him no end of trouble? A woman who had mixed up gratitude and love?

The closer they'd gotten to civilization, the more alert he'd become, his sharp gaze sweeping the terrain carefully, his long strides controlled, as though he could shift direction in a split second. She could almost see an assault rifle slung over his shoulder instead of Philip's battered duffel. Slowly, gradually, he was becoming the walking weapon he'd once been.

When they were finished with their meager meal of stale bread and tepid water, she wadded up the wrappings and shoved everything into her tote. In a few minutes they would have to be on the move again.

Not yet, she thought. It's too soon.

She took a broken breath and curved her mouth into a smile. "I wish I could have seen you without your sexy whiskers," she teased, popping a peanut-butter miniature into her mouth.

"Take a look at some old newspaper clippings. My face was spread all over the front page for weeks."

Cutter had never thought that watching someone eat would make his blood run faster. But Regan wasn't just eating that small morsel of chocolate. She was making passionate love to it.

Her smudged eyes were half-closed in her pale face. An expression of rapture hovered over her mouth.

"Maybe I'll do that."

Tension knifed at the corners of his mouth. His voice took on the clipped edge he'd all but abandoned. "Forget I said that. It's a stupid idea. When I'm gone, I want you to forget I ever existed."

Regan made herself smile, but inside, she was slowly being shredded into bits. "I won't change my mind about you, no matter what I read."

"A lot of people did, including most of my friends. I'm not sure there was enough of my marriage left to lose."

Regan had a feeling that was the first time he'd admitted as much. Maybe he would find some small measure of peace in the admission. "Surely some people stuck by you."

"Some. Hank, my partner, a coupla guys who worked with me on the Greaves case. My dad's old partner."

He stood up and walked to the edge of the trail where it sloped into the shallow ravine. "My sister came to the trial. She wanted to visit me after I went inside, but I wouldn't let her."

"Why not?"

He bent to pick up a jagged stone. His fingers tested the edge before he hurled it across the shallow pocket in the earth, where it crashed into the opposite slope, sending chunks of dirt falling into the rocky ravine.

"I didn't want her to see her big brother in that place."

Regan understood, and her heart went out to him. Jake was a man of fierce pride, a man used to being in control, being strong. It must have hurt terribly to bend his will to the control of others.

"What about your daughter?" she asked softly.

He wasn't a man who loved easily, she knew, but when he did, he loved totally, fiercely, loyally. Carole Ann was very lucky to have such a man as a father. Someday she would believe that, too—if Jake kept the lines open.

He dropped his gaze, but not before Regan saw a terrible sorrow in his eyes. "I have to let her go, Regan," he said in a low dead voice. "It's killing me, but I have no choice.

You . . . you're the only one who knows I'm alive. If anyone else knew . . ."

She heard the slicing frustration in his voice and knew then the heavy burden of guilt and pain he would always carry on those broad shoulders. Not because he was an evil man and deserved to be punished, but because he had tried to take care of too many people, the people he loved.

"I'm sorry, Jake," she murmured. "I'm so sorry."

"So am I."

"I love you, Jake Cutter. Please remember that."

"I can't, Regan. I can't take anything from this place with me."

He turned to look at her, his eyes dark and tormented, his mouth stiff. "Please understand. That's the only way I can stay strong."

Too filled with pain to speak, Regan clamped her trembling lip between her teeth and nodded. In every way that mattered, they were saying goodbye. When they parted at the bottom of the slope, they would never see each other again.

Jake grabbed their packs. "We've gotta go. The fire's too close."

He helped her to her feet, then shouldered their packs. "Stay close. We have to move fast."

"Yes, all right."

Regan wanted to fling herself on him and beg him to stay. She wanted to scream in pain. She couldn't do any of those things.

Cutter turned away before he found himself reaching for her again. Before he wrapped his arms around her and buried his face in the perfumed silk of her hair.

The closer they got to town, the more he wanted to throw her over his shoulder and haul her off to exile with him. The fact that he couldn't was ripping open the holes inside him that Regan had begun to fill.

They walked quickly, angling along the top of a shallow ravine. Only a thick stand of pine and underbrush stood between them and the flames. The smoke grew denser, making it hard to breathe. The crackling roar was terrifyingly loud.

Regan lost track of time. Jake pushed faster, until they were moving at a trot. Exhausted, she concentrated on putting one foot in front of the other. She could see the reflection of the flames on the smoke cloud overhead. The wind was hot and getting hotter. Just as the trail curved sharply around a thick stand of sage and chaparral, she heard something crashing through brush on her left. Five deer charged toward her, their hooves making clicking sounds against the rocks. Driven by fear, they passed so close that she could see the crazed look in the eyes of the smallest.

Behind them, she saw smoke and whirling bits of flaming leaves showering onto the tinder-dry brush. The chaparral exploded into flames, the heat creating a maelstrom of ash and cinders and choking smoke.

"Jake!" she screamed, glancing around frantically for shelter. The noise was terrible, disorienting her. Flames shot higher than the trees. Smoke roiled upward.

Cutter's trained eye searched for cover. He saw an outcropping of rock ahead, a shelter of sorts. It was close, but they had a shot.

"C'mon! This way!" he shouted over the roar. "Run!"

Half-blinded by the stinging smoke, Regan obeyed instantly. Her breath was a tortured sound in her ears. Her legs protested, threatening to knot into cramps with each step she took.

In her haste to reach him, she stepped where she shouldn't. The smooth soles of her sneakers skidded on the loose gravel, and her right foot slipped off the trail.

She fell, tumbling crazily down the slope of the ravine as though she were a rag doll, her scream trailing behind her. Her foot slammed into a large jagged rock torquing her knee sideways. She felt something tear, followed by a searing pain.

Jackknifed in agony, she hugged her knee to her chest, oblivious to anything but the white-hot throbbing beneath the skin.

Over the crackle of the flames she heard Jake's voice calling her name. Dimly, through a haze of nausea, she was aware that he was making his way down the slope, slipping and sliding in his haste.

She sobbed out his name, struggling to keep from surrendering to the weakness taking hold of her. Through an ear-bashing rush of sound, she felt the crush of denim-clad legs against the backs of her bare thighs. The hard shelter of his wide chest. The strength of his arm protecting her.

"Take small breaths," he ordered, his voice stripped raw. "It's going to get hot." He tucked her face into the curve of his shoulder.

The noise was deafening, a crackling spitting roar that pounded at her ears until she wanted to scream. A hot wind worse than any Santa Ana tore past them. Burning cinders and ash and bits of gravel churned around them. She felt Cutter flinch as he took the worst of it on his back.

The roar grew terrifyingly close, and the earth seemed to rumble. With a hot whoosh, the air seemed to be sucked from her lungs. She struggled to breathe as Cutter's arm tightened, pinning her against him. Her vision began to blur. Her throat closed.

Just when she knew she was going to suffocate, the roar began fading. She inhaled deeply, greedy for air. Still gripped by terror, she was afraid to move.

"Is...is it gone?" she whispered when her throat relaxed.

Cutter raised his head and listened. The roar was definitely fading, but the smoke was still thick and choking. Spot fires burned all around, but the hard bare ground bordering the ravine had provided a natural firebreak, sparing them.

"Better give it a few more minutes to make sure." Blood was trickling into his eye. He wiped it away with the back of his hand, leaving a long red smear on his temple.

"Thank God," she murmured, closing her eyes.

Cutter sat up and brushed the tangled hair from her face. Fear made his stomach burn and his mouth dry. She was deathly pale, and beads of moisture dampened her brow. She looked so fragile, so vulnerable.

"Where does it hurt, honey? Talk to me."

She tried to answer, but the pain was too terrible.

"Regan, tell me where it hurts."

"My knee," she managed to gasp.

"Let go of your leg, honey, so I can look at it. I can't see what's wrong when you're hugging yourself like that."

"Mmm?"

"Regan, you have to let go of your knee."

She tried to smile, but she didn't think she succeeded. Too woozy to try again, she did as she was told. Even that small movement drove stinging needles into her joint.

She closed her eyes. "You'll miss me, won't you?" Her tongue was so thick, it was difficult to make the words come out right.

Cutter felt his gut tear. "You're in shock," he said carefully.

She tried to protest, but the words wouldn't come. Her eyelids seemed terribly heavy, and she let them drift shut.

"I'm sorry I'm...such a klutz." Her lashes fluttered. Her fingers played with the hair on his arm. "What are we going to do now?"

"First you're going to put your arms around my neck, and then I'm going to carry you down the road to Tatum's Bend."

Regan clutched at his arms, but her fingers were strangely clumsy. "You can't do that. It's not safe. What if someone sees you? Recognizes you? I couldn't stand it if you had to go back to prison because of me."

He bent his head and kissed her. It was the gentlest of kisses, so light she barely felt the pressure of his mouth.

"You promised not to worry about me, remember?"

Her head lolled drunkenly as she tried to tilt it back enough to see his face. His hard dear fiercely proud face.

"I don't think I'm ever going to stop missing you," she said in a sad soft whisper.

Regan tried to concentrate, to control her breathing. "I wish..." Her voice broke. She licked her dry lips, then tried again. What she had to say was important. "I wish I could give you a child. If I could...if I could, I'd tell him every day how brave and honorable and decent his father is."

"Regan, don't." Cutter felt as though he had suddenly been sliced open and left to bleed to death.

Her ashen lips curved into a trembling smile. "I wish you'd loved me just a little. If you had, you wouldn't feel so alone when you're in one of those horrible little countries, trying to find a reason to stay alive."

She fought to stay awake, but the ground began to spin around her. The last thing she heard before she slipped into the swirling voice inside her head was the harsh voice of a man in terrible pain, crying out her name. A man with tears slowly sliding down his hard tormented face.

Regan opened her eyes and saw a blaze of white. White ceiling, white curtain, white walls. An intravenous drip was spiraling down to a needle in her arm.

A hospital? Was she in a hospital somewhere? In the city?

Her mind was sluggish, her body limp and terribly heavy, as though she were coming off a two-day drunk—except, of course, she didn't drink.

A frown slowly formed between her eyebrows. She turned her head, her lashes fluttering in mild curiosity. Nothing seemed to matter much. She felt empty, drained of energy.

"Welcome back to the world, lovely lady."

The man sitting by the bed was dressed in hand-tailored banker's gray worsted. He stood up and took her hand in his, dominating the small cubicle with three hundred pounds of dignity and self-assurance.

"Philip?" Her voice was a croak, her throat paper dry. "Is it really you?"

His thin mouth curved into the clipped edges of his salt-and-pepper beard. "As soon as the ranger called me to say that the fire had destroyed my cabin and I realized you were missing, I chartered a plane. I was at the aid station when they brought you in. Your folks will be here tonight."

Disoriented and more than a little fuzzy around the edges, Regan lifted her head off the pillow. The room began to spin in crazy circles, and she let her head fall.

"I hope they weren't too worried."

One silver eyebrow quirked. "We were all worried, Regan. Even your clients. Pictures of the fire were all over the six o'clock news."

She licked her lips. The lower one felt cracked. "I feel woozy."

"The paramedics gave you a shot for the pain before they put a splint on your knee."

"Where am I?"

"Now there's an original question!" His shrewd blue eyes twinkled down at her, but the patrician forehead under the carefully brushed silver pompadour was furrowed with concern. "You're in Tatum's Bend Community Hospital. Exactly how you got here is the question a lot of people are waiting to ask—including a half-dozen reporters prowling the waiting room."

Regan blinked, confusion gradually replacing her drug-induced lethargy. "Reporters?"

"Yes. Seems you're hot news, Reggie, you and your convict rescuer. Heroics under desperate circumstances, two strangers trapped together, an ex-cop convicted killer and a beautiful long-legged social worker. Sensational stuff. One of them has a picture of said convict sagging to his knees after paramedics took you from his arms. Only he knows how many miles he carried you. Enough to make him pass out as soon as you were safe, however."

Her frown turned into a strangled gasp. "Oh, my God, where is he? Where's Jake?" She sat up, then cried out and grabbed for the knee propped on a nest of pillows.

"Easy, baby," Philip said as his large plump hands eased her shaking body back onto the pillows. "Along with a few other things, like torn cartilage and a bruised back, you're suffering from exhaustion."

Regan waited for the pain to pass, then clutched at Philip's arm. Her eyelids threatened to close, and she held them open by pure willpower.

"I want Jake. Where's Jake?"

His mouth sobered. "Back in his cell by now, I imagine."

"Oh no, no. What happened?"

"Just as they were loading the two of you into the ambulance, one of the guards supervising the inmate volunteers, a Neanderthal by the name of Rhottman, spotted your friend and insisted that he be returned to Donovan immediately."

An expression of distaste crossed his face. "Last I saw of him, your friend was sitting in the back of a sheriff's cruiser, his face covered with blood, his hands cuffed behind him. He looked like he was in bad shape."

Regan shivered. Jake, back in prison.

Oh, Jake, she thought sadly. Why didn't you go when you had the chance? Why?

"He saved my life instead of his own."

"I don't understand."

Her chin angled into an obstinate line. "You have to help him, Philip. There's no one else. I don't care what else you have to do, *you have to help him*."

Philip's eyebrows rose. "In the eight or nine years since we've been friends, you've never once asked me for a favor, which is probably why I'm so crazy about you." He cleared his throat. "I take it this man is something special?"

Regan thought about the tormented look in Jake's lone-wolf eyes when he'd vowed that nothing in this world mattered to him but his freedom.

"Very special," she said, pain washing her voice. "More special than he knows."

"I see." Philip returned to the chair and took out a leather-bound notebook and a gold pen. "In that case, maybe you'd better start at the beginning."

It was difficult to pace with a full leg cast and crutches, but since Philip had left the beachfront hotel to drive out to the prison to represent Jake at his disciplinary hearing hours before, Regan had done a good job of wearing a rut in the plush carpet.

Two weeks had passed since Philip had agreed to take Jake's case, ten days of playing power poker with the warden, of calling in markers in Sacramento, of engaging in the elegant street fighting that had made Philip a wealthy man.

As soon as he returned, she pounced. "What was the board's ruling?"

Philip closed the door and flung his hand-tooled calfskin briefcase onto the bed. "Ninety days in punitive isolation. I imagine his time has already started."

"What in blazes does that mean? Punitive isolation?"

Moving gracefully for such a large man, he crossed to the dresser, uncapped the bottle of twelve-year-old scotch he'd given into Regan's care that morning and poured himself three fingers, which he proceeded to swallow without a grimace. Fortified, he said tersely, "What it means, Reggie, is this. Cutter hit a guard, which is unequivocally against the rules in every prison in this country. The man had to be punished, or a dangerous precedent would have been set. I could only do so much, even for you."

He refilled the glass, added ice from the bucket and sat down in the room's only chair. He looked hot and tired and definitely not in the mood to placate a half-frantic, definitely bullheaded, clearly-in-love woman.

"For heaven's sake, Philip, Jake had a damned good reason for hitting that guard! I would have done the same thing myself."

"I have no doubt of that at all."

Regan's cheeks began to flame, putting color into her face for the first time since she had been released from the hospital six days earlier.

"His parole?"

"Granted, although it was a near thing. Rhottman denied everything. Claims Cutter was trying to escape."

"Bastard."

Slowly, still awkward on the crutches, she made her way to the bed. Frowning at the pain, she eased herself onto the mattress and dropped the crutches.

"I still can't understand why the other men didn't come forward to testify, especially that man Chacon."

Philip snorted. "That's because you're a nice middle-class lady who's never done hard time. There's a code of silence, Regan. A con handles his own problems in his own way. No matter what happens to him, he never snitches, especially on a guard." He waited the right number of beats, then added softly, "Otherwise, he's as good as dead."

Her eyes widened until they dominated her too-pale face. "But Jake—"

"Jake didn't bring the charges. Rhottman did. In that case, Jake has a right to defend himself."

Regan drew an explosive breath. "I hate it that he's in that place, Philip. Every time I think about him there, confined, tormented, I want to hit something."

"He's tough, Regan. He's survived three years. He'll survive till his parole, especially now that the warden has agreed to transfer Rhottman to another cell-block." He drank deeply, and the ice cubes rattled in the glass.

Regan stared at the snowy cast encasing her sprained knee. In six weeks the cast would come off, and she would be as good as new. Such a short time, really, unless a person was spending it in hell.

The weight of her pain settled hard inside her. She had never felt so helpless and so hurting, not even when she'd miscarried.

"Tell me about isolation, Philip."

He shook his head. "It's better if you don't know."

"You know I hate it when you try to baby me." Her voice took on a warning edge. Philip scowled, then shook his head in weary surrender. He'd lost too many battles with Regan Delaney when she'd been in a combative mood.

"Okay, you asked for it." His glass hit the table with a clunk. "Isolation is a concrete cell containing a bunk, a toilet and a sink. The only light comes in through a small barred window in the steel door. He's allowed out for one hour a day to shower and shave and exercise in a small concrete enclosure. Other than that, he's locked in alone."

As Philip talked, Regan grew whiter and whiter. Her hands twisted into small fists in her lap. Her breathing came to a dead halt, then began again, quicker, driven by pain.

Naturally empathetic under his cynical facade, Philip felt his throat close. He didn't want to go on, but he knew she would insist.

"It's supposed to make a prisoner reflect on the errors of his ways. A lot of people think it's a cruel and unusual punishment."

Regan felt frozen, her face, her hands, her heart. All the warmth seemed to have been sucked from the room, leaving it ice cold.

"Not ninety days, Philip," she whispered. "No one can take ninety days of that."

"He has to. He doesn't have a choice."

"But he did! That's what makes it so unfair. He could have left me close to town, someplace where I was certain to be found. If he had, he would be in Mexico by now. Free."

She ran her icy hand over the cast. The plaster was rough, like Jake's beard under her caressing fingers. Would she ever see that hard strong jaw without its sexy beard? Would she ever see his rare smile again?

"Reggie, are you all right? Should I get one of your pain pills?"

"I'm fine." Her voice sounded hollow.

"You should be in bed, and you know it. In spite of what you think, young lady, you're not invincible. You need rest."

Regan acknowledged Philip's gruff concern with a stiff parody of her usual heart-melting grin.

"Don't fuss, Philip. The Delaneys are good peasant stock. It takes a lot to bring one of us down."

Outside, the surf pounded the shoreline. Gulls flew overhead, screaming raucous insults to the sunbathers below. The sun was baking hot, just the way she craved it, but she was still cold inside.

"Did you see him after the hearing? How is he?"

Philip's grumpy expression softened. He could never stay angry around Regan. "Actually he's holding up better than you are. The man has steel behind those cold eyes. And a damned good brain. He should go into law."

"If you're so impressed, why didn't you defend him three years ago?"

Philip rubbed his hand across his chin. Regan recognized the telltale sign of dented pride, and she cast him a come-clean look.

"All right, so I was wrong. I thought the guy had a macho-cop complex. Turns out he made a mistake in judgment, that's all."

"Did you tell him that?"

"Hell, yes. I've always prided myself on my ability to admit I'm wrong, a quality, I might add, you would do well to cultivate." Something in his expression aroused her curiosity.

"Out with it, Philip."

"With what, darling?"

Regan lowered her chin and held his gaze until he confessed grudgingly, "When I first went to see him, he refused my services. None too gently, I might add. Said he wasn't interested in telling his story to a man who thought he was dirty. If you ask me, the man has too much pride for his own good."

They were in perfect agreement on that point. "I want to see him, Philip."

"You can't. Not until he comes out of isolation. Even then, you have to go through channels. Visiting privileges are strictly regulated."

"You said attorneys have unlimited access to their clients. You could get me in."

"Regan—"

"Tell them I'm your assistant."

With a from-the-depths-of-his-soul sigh, Philip pushed his bulk out of the inadequate chair and crossed the room to open his case. Inside was a bag of peanut-butter miniatures.

"He asked me to buy you these." Very gently, his blue eyes dark with compassion, he placed them in her hands.

Regan smiled tenderly as she hugged the bag to her chest, her heart aching with the memory of Cutter's tawny head resting against her breasts the last time they'd made love.

"Did he send me a message?"

She'd sent a letter with Philip, telling Jake how much she loved him, how deeply she believed in him. So far, there hadn't been an answer.

He nodded, his expression uncharacteristically somber. "He said to tell you that he was holding you to your promise to get on with your life."

Regan remembered each and every one of the words they'd said to each other. So few, really. Was that all she would ever have of him? Words imprinted on her memory? Passion imprinted on her body?

No, she thought. I can't let him go. I can't.

Remember your promise.

Her fingers crushed the soft chocolate candies until her knuckles threatened to pop. "Why is he doing this, Philip? Why?"

Love, Philip thought in disgust. Who the hell needs it?

The bedsprings groaned under his weight as he sat down next to her and slipped an arm around her shoulders.

Philip Sinclair was not a sentimental man. His years in the blood-and-guts mire of often brutal court battles had made him jaded and cynical. He'd seen too much to believe that anyone these days did anything out of selfless concern.

Except for Regan Delaney.

Except for Jake Cutter.

"You'll have to ask him, Regan, because I can only hazard a guess. But this I do know. Jacob Cutter has a remarkable will, and a capacity for obstinacy that matches it. Once he's made up his mind, nothing, not even God Almighty, can change it."

Eleven

"Checkmate."

Clarence Eldridge tossed Cutter's king onto the bunk and grinned. "You ain't concentratin' worth a damn, man. I'm beginnin' to believe you just love to lose."

"Like hell!"

Cutter swept the chess pieces off the small board and surged to his feet. Slamming his hands into his back pockets, he began to pace, his naturally long strides restricted by the narrow space between the back wall and the bars. At least this wasn't isolation....

He stopped at the bars and stared across at the opposite tier. But instead of caged men he saw Regan, smiling up at him by the stream, a flush from his lovemaking on her perfect breasts. She'd been breathtaking at that moment, alive with the kind of inner beauty that defied words, the kind that touched a man in the deepest part of his soul.

Eldridge came up behind him and touched his shoulder. "Eight more months, man. You'll make it."

Cutter sighed. "Yeah, I'll make it." Restless and edgy, he walked to his bunk and sat down. He picked up a book, opened it, put it down again. He lit a cigarette, smoked it without enjoyment, put it out. He stood and walked to the bars again.

Eldridge hoisted himself to the top bunk and began swinging his powerful weight lifter's legs. His black pock-marked face was twisted into a somber preoccupied look.

"You gonna see her when you get out?"

Cutter stared straight ahead. "No."

"'Cause you think you ain't good enough for her, that it?"

Cutter turned and leaned against the bars. "Look at me, man. I'm a beat-up ex-cop who's about to become an ex-con. My ex-wife is going to make me fight for access to my daughter, which will cost money I don't have."

Too tense to settle, he began pacing again. "Not to mention the fact that I've still got debts from my trial, a load of garbage heaped on my name, a lot of years in grad school before I can hope to make enough to support a wife. That's some package to offer to a lady, don't you think?"

He stopped at the bars. He was so damn tired of living this way. Of fighting every day to hang on to his self-esteem. Of trying not to think of the life he might have had with Regan if things had been different. If *he'd* been different.

Eldridge nodded his shaved head. "Hmm, now I get your drift, man. You got to be the head honcho in this twosome, that right?"

Cutter walked to the sink and stuck his head under the tap to take a long drink. "No, that's not right," he returned irritably. "But I'm sure as hell not going to put my problems on the woman I . . . on Regan."

"'Course, I ain't no expert, but it seems to me it don't make no difference if you got love between you."

"Regan doesn't love me." His voice was rough with the need to make himself remember that fact. "She had gratitude and love all mixed up for a while, but she's a smart lady. I'm sure it didn't take her long to figure it out.''

"You know that for a fact, do you?''

Cutter caught the skeptical look in his friend's eyes and scowled. ''Hell, yes, I know. She's special. She deserves a man she won't be ashamed to introduce as her husband.''

He stretched out on his bunk and folded his arms under his head, raising one knee and trying to ignore the tension knotting his belly.

That was the worst of it, knowing she might someday be hurt because of him. He could handle physical pain and frustration and the never-ending agony of living the rest of his life as an ex-convict. But it would kill him to hurt Regan.

He ran a hand down his face and turned onto his side. Eight more months, he said to himself. Two hundred and forty-two days. A lifetime.

"Yo, Cutter. Your attorney's here,'' called a Latin-accented voice from the walkway outside the bars. Garcia was one of the more decent guards.

"Sinclair?''

"Beats me, man,'' Garcia said, opening the cell door and stepping back to let Cutter precede him. ''I just come to fetch ya.''

"Now, you're sure you know what to do?'' Regan tugged nervously on the collar of her emerald silk shirt and wet her dry lips one more time.

Beside her, Philip grunted in long-suffering patience. ''As soon as Cutter gets here, I'm supposed to excuse myself and go to the men's room.''

"And stay there, remember? I warned you to bring a book.''

Philip sighed. ''Only for you, my darling Regan,'' he muttered.

Trying not to fidget, Regan straightened her collar again. The room was nearly full. Long wooden tables were crowded into neat rows, inmates on one side, visitors on the other. An overweight, red-faced guard with greasy black hair sat at a small table by the visitors' entrance, checking badges and entering the name of each visitor next to the name of the inmate.

Everything was regimented, from the articles that could be brought into the room, such as candy, to the clothing that couldn't be worn by visitors. No blue denim like those the inmates wore, no khaki like that worn by the guards. In the case of a riot, the instructions explained baldly, the guards needed to know immediately who was who.

But the worst had been the sound of the barred doors opening and closing behind them as she and Philip had been led by a bored guard through bleak airless corridors to the visiting room. The hard final clang of metal locking into metal still shuddered inside her.

How many times had Jake heard that sound? How long would he hear it in his nightmares after he was finally allowed to leave this place?

She took a long slow breath and tried to calm her galloping nerves. For weeks she'd been planning this visit, changing her mind almost daily about her hairstyle, her outfit, the amount of makeup she should wear.

She'd finally settled on tailored chic: a long-sleeved blouse, a straight skirt that showed off her legs, high-heeled pumps that flattered her ankles.

After hours of experimentation in front of the mirror, she'd finally decided she looked most tempting with her hair piled loosely on top of her head.

She wasn't playing fair, but then, Jake hadn't played fair, either, sending a message by Philip instead of writing to her.

She intended to knock him on his ear and, while he was reeling, slip under his guard. Or so she had told herself at least a dozen times during the flight to San Diego.

Now she was having second thoughts. Seeing the barbed wire curled angrily atop the towering concrete wall, feeling the tension that permeated this room, absorbing the hard angry looks on the faces of the men she'd seen, the rigid, dehumanizing rules and regulations even for visiting privileges—those things had given her a new understanding of the kind of life Jake had been forced to lead in this place. Regan wet her lips again. Why was it taking so long? Didn't anyone care that Jake had someone waiting?

The shuttle taking them from the visitors' parking lot to the main gate had been late, cutting into precious visiting time. Then, for what seemed like hours, she'd had to wait in line to have her identity checked and her purse searched. After that, she'd had to fill out a form in triplicate, have her hand stamped, a badge issued, her belongings stowed in a locker.

She glanced over her shoulder. "I'm going to talk to the guard. Maybe he can find out what's taking so long." Before she could leave her chair, Philip clamped a hand around her wrist.

"Prison cells don't have phones, Reggie. Someone has to track him down. Besides, you don't want to make the guy mad. It could go hard on Jake later."

Just then the door at the end of the room opened. Dressed as she'd first seen him in worn jeans and a faded blue shirt, Cutter hesitated on the threshold, his sharp gaze searching the room.

She noticed his eyes first, narrowed with suspicion, keenly curious, shadowed with the kind of fatigue that comes only from months of unrelieved suffering.

He was thinner, his cheeks hollowed into gauntness. His hair was haphazardly brushed, falling forward in a sexy tangle begging for her fingers to smooth it into order. There were new strands of gray mixed in with the myriad shades of blond.

Their eyes collided, and for an instant she saw a savage joy settle into the depths of his before his face went completely blank.

Three long impatient strides brought him to the table where she and Philip sat alone. There was a restless quality about his lean body and a controlled look around his mouth. Scraped clean of whiskers, his jaw was set in an intimidating line.

Regan felt the fires of her love for him lick hotter. This big gaunt, obviously suffering man was part of her. Now she just had to convince him of that.

Ignoring her completely, he pinned his angry gaze on Philip. "You'd better have a damn good reason for this."

Philip returned Cutter's challenging stare impassively. "I see that isolation hasn't soothed your temper."

Cutter snorted. "You got that right." The two men exchanged glances that each clearly understood. Regan didn't.

"Don't blame Philip," she said, drawing a quick furious look from those proud eyes. "This was my idea."

The air around them felt alive. "I don't want you here, Regan." His voice was deep and husky, like a man suddenly out of breath.

"That wasn't the message I got. You told me to get on with my life, and that's what I'm doing. We have unfinished business, you and I."

He scowled, but the hard look around his mouth eased. "Regan—"

"Take my advice, man," Philip interrupted smoothly, his cultured voice laced with wry amusement. "Save your breath. I've been through this same scene with her, and you can see the result. The lady can be quite…formidable when she wants something badly enough."

He pushed back his chair and lumbered to his feet, then extended his hand. After a split second's hesitation, Cutter took it.

Philip looked at Cutter's hard-hewn face, lined even more cruelly by suffering now, and studied the sharp intelligent eyes darkened by the kind of hunger that comes from deep punishing loneliness.

He thought about the ninety days this man had spent alone in the dark because he'd tried to spare someone else's pain. He thought about the news photo of this man crumbling into the dust after carrying a woman he scarcely knew through smoke and flame to save her life. He thought about second chances, those who deserved them, those who didn't.

"You still planning to go to graduate school when you're paroled?" Philip asked when the handshake ended.

Cutter inclined his head in a stiff nod. "If I get accepted."

"Applied anywhere yet?"

"UCLA."

The attorney frowned. "We have grad schools in the Bay Area, too."

Cutter looked at him impassively. Philip met his gaze steadily. They were both powerful confident men, Regan thought, watching them take each other's measure.

"You'll need a job to pay the bills. I still need another skilled investigator on my staff. Name your own hours. Work around your classes."

As though he couldn't help himself, Cutter shifted his gaze to Regan's flushed face. "I'll think about it."

Spirits soaring, Regan shot Philip a pointed look.

The attorney smoothed his silk tie and carefully buttoned his suit coat. "I'm supposed to excuse myself so that you two can be alone." He patted Regan's shoulder, then turned and walked away.

Cutter watched him go for a moment, then slowly shifted his gaze to her face.

Knees shaking, she stood up and walked around the table, conscious of heads turning her way. She blocked out the curious eyes, the nervous flutters in her stomach, the noise in the room, everything but Jake.

"The rules say we can kiss hello and goodbye."

She saw him struggle to resist, saw him surrender. With a heavy sigh, he took her shoulders and pulled her toward him. The moment their lips met, Regan felt alive again.

Oblivious to the long list of rules, forgetting her determination to remain in control, she felt herself melt against him. This was Jake, the man she loved. She knew the taste of him, the feel of him, even the sound of his breathing.

Her arms started to reach for him, but he stepped quickly away, his gaze flicking toward the guard. Pain seared her. How it must gall him to know he could be punished just for letting a kiss go on too long.

Flushed and furious, she returned to her seat.

After a moment's hesitation, Cutter pulled out a chair and sat down, too. Even as he did, he knew he was making a mistake, one he would pay for in sweat drenched nights and lonely days. But he just couldn't seem to make himself walk away. The intoxicating lure of her was too strong. His loneliness was too deep.

They sat in silence, their eyes locked. Now that she was here, actually close enough to touch him, she didn't know where to begin. She was so aware of the too-thin hollowed-eyed man across three feet of scarred table that she could scarcely draw breath.

"I had a whole speech memorized," she murmured. "All about you and why I love you so much."

"You don't take orders very well. I told you to forget me." His voice was rough.

Regan folded her hands in front of her. His were pressed flat. She longed to hold him, to caress away those terrible lines, to bathe him in her love until he forgot this place.

"Actually I don't take orders at all. My folks said I had a redhead's temperament under all this brown hair."

Her words drew Cutter's gaze to her hair. He noticed that she was wearing it up in some kind of loose style, with little tendrils curling over the nape of her neck. With one hand he could tumble that sophisticated style into wild disarray over her shoulders. He told himself to forget it.

"I don't want you here, Regan."

"Straight ahead, to the point, clearly combative." She nodded, her lips curving into a smile. "No wonder you and Philip get along so well."

Cutter tried not to notice the way her lower lip took on an extra fullness when she smiled. Or the way her long brown lashes made her eyes look softly provocative, even in the harsh artificial light.

Regan saw his jaw harden and decided a change of subject was in order. "You've lost weight."

She worried the slim gold chain around her neck with nervous fingers. His eyes followed the quick little movements for an instant before shifting to the swell of her breasts.

"So have you."

Regan was ridiculously pleased that he'd noticed. She'd only dropped a few pounds, not enough for anyone to tell, really—unless he carried her memory in his head the way she carried his.

"You've shaved."

"I usually do."

This wasn't the man who had made love to her by the stream. That man had been tender, loving, even vulnerable, not like this daunting frozen-faced man with bitter lines around his mouth and unreadable eyes.

"You saved my life," she said softly. "Thank you."

"Your friend Sinclair saved mine. We're even."

He was trying to tell her that she didn't owe him anything. Was that why he thought she'd come? If that was true, that would explain the hard glint in his eyes.

She leaned forward, trying to erase some of the distance between them. If only she were free to touch him, she thought. Then he would know that gratitude had nothing to do with her reasons for coming.

"Philip is going to rebuild his cabin."

Cutter thought she could get more expression into her eyes than anyone he'd ever known. At the moment they were shimmering with the kind of promises a man usually saw only in his dreams.

"Good for Philip." His voice was oddly scratchy. Regan took that as a good sign.

"He's offered to let me use it whenever I want. I told him September twelfth. I want you to come with me."

Jake felt the hole in his belly rip wider. September 12 was the day of his release. He knew what she was offering. He knew he would give his immortal soul to accept.

"No."

"Why not?" She stretched her hand across the table to cover his. When he couldn't stand it any longer, he turned his palm up and entwined their fingers.

Heartbeat quickening, she returned the pressure. "God, Jake, I was so afraid you wouldn't let me touch you. I've missed touching you. I've missed the way you look when you're trying not to smile. Mostly I've missed the way I feel safe when I'm with you."

Cutter struggled with emotions he didn't dare name. He was existing in a living hell without her, but having her so close and not being able to touch her the way he wanted to was worse.

"Don't come here again, Regan. I won't see you if you do."

She felt a moment of panic. He wanted her. She could see it in his eyes. And if he wanted her, he could come to love her. All they needed was a chance.

"I know you think I'm just grateful to you, and maybe you still think no woman could want you after... after all this." She waved her free hand in the general direction of the guard's desk. "But you're wrong. I want you, and I need you."

Cutter saw the vulnerability come into her eyes. He had seen that look before, on the day she'd told him about her husband's mistress.

He hated himself for putting that look there. He hated the fact that he had no choice. For the first time he knew what it was like to cry inside. It was worse than bleeding.

He folded her hand between his. He knew this would be the last time he would ever look into those warm smiling eyes, the last time he would feel her skin against his, the last time he would hear the music of her voice.

"Be quite a minute and listen to me," he ordered. "There's something I have to say."

Regan felt a shiver pass through her. This man was more lonesome, more emotionally scarred, than anyone she'd ever known. Whatever demons were driving him, she had a feeling he'd faced them alone for a long time.

"If you're going to tell me that I don't love you, I'm not going to listen."

"You'll listen. Otherwise I'll get up and walk out."

His threat was real. He would do as he said. Jake would always do as he said.

"All right, but that doesn't mean I don't get my say when you're finished." Her chin angled, and her eyes flashed in rebellion.

For a moment Jake couldn't breathe. She was a whirlwind of emotion, soft and loving one minute, fiery and challenging the next. Life with her would be exciting and fun and so damn wonderful he felt dizzy thinking about it.

He started to smile, but an angry shout to his right diverted him. At the next table a con he didn't know pounded the table with his fist, shouting obscenities at a fragile-looking white-faced woman across from him. A look of pain bled into her wounded blue eyes, and she began to cry, harsh tormented sobs shaking her small frame.

The guard quickly got to his feet, but before he could intercede, the guy slammed out of the room.

"That poor woman," Regan said softly, watching the sobbing woman hurry toward the opposite door, her face flaming.

Cutter went cold inside. That poor woman could be Regan someday. All it would take would be a moment's uncontrolled rage, a few vicious unthinking words. After years in this stinking place, he was capable of both.

Cutter pulled his hands from Regan's and rested them on his thighs. He made his voice cold and unfeeling.

"You have a soft heart, Regan. Too soft. You want to take care of everyone you meet. But I have no desire to be one of your reclamation projects. I don't need your charity, and I sure as hell don't need my life arranged like I was some dumb kid off the streets."

She flinched. "I'm not—"

"Yes, you are. Look at what you've done already—cajoled your high-powered friend to lean on the warden for me, arranged a job—"

"I didn't!" she protested heatedly. "That was Philip's idea."

The sardonic look he gave her spoke volumes. "You've got this romantic notion that I'm some kind of heroic victim, a lost soul. A few kisses, and all your protective juices are flowing. Poor guy, you tell yourself. He needs someone. He needs me."

"You do need me," she said in a low urgent tone. "Just the way I need you. Everyone needs someone."

Cutter thought of the long empty hours of the night that hadn't seemed as lonely when she'd been curled up next to him. He thought of the hard days ahead without the sound of her bubbling laughter to give him courage. He thought of the violent sound of a man's fist slamming against wood. It could just as easily have been his fist. He couldn't take that chance.

Better to hurt her now, while all they had between them was a few memories, than to hurt her far worse later.

"I don't need anyone. And I sure as hell don't want anyone to need me."

Regan saw the glint of some terrible twisting emotion in his eyes. Something was wrong; something didn't feel right. Jake was saying one thing, but the pain in his eyes was saying something else.

"I don't think that's true," she said slowly. "I think you do have feelings for me, and you've been hiding them because of your pride, because you don't think you have anything to offer me."

He leaned back and angled one arm over the back of the chair. He would rather have taken a public beating from a dozen brutes like Rhottman than say the words that had to be said, in the way he had to say them.

"I have feelings, all right. It's called lust, Regan. I've got the hots for you. But that's all we have, you and me. Terrific sex." He glanced toward the guard, then deliberately trained his icy eyes on her breasts. It was the crudest kind of insult. Regan could scarcely breathe. Heat surged into her cheeks.

"Why are you doing this?" she asked in a nearly soundless tone. "Are you trying to make me hate you?"

His mouth flattened. "Now why would I do that?" The lost look in her eyes was shredding him inside. If he weren't so certain he was doing this to protect her, he would have been on his knees in front of a room full of strangers begging her to forgive him.

Regan sat frozen, staring at him in silence. She'd seen that look on his face before, she thought, frantically searching through her memories of their time together.

It had been on that last afternoon, right before the fire caught them. He'd been saying goodbye then, too.

I love you, Jake Cutter. Please remember that.

I can't take anything with me. That's the only way I can stay strong.

He'd said something else that day. That he was letting his daughter go, even though it was killing him. Because he loved her.

Regan took a slow ragged breath, and got to her feet.

Cutter was so certain she was going to walk away that he was taken completely by surprise when she walked quickly around the table to stand next to him.

Before he could react, she framed his face in her hands and whispered firmly, "I'm not wrong about you, Jake Cutter. You need me so much it scares you. And you know what else I've just figured out? You're in love with me. I just hope it's not too late when you finally get around to admitting it.''

Before he could do more than stare at her in shock, she bent her head and touched her lips to his in a chaste kiss. This time she was the one who turned and walked away.

"What's wrong with you, man? Someone make a move on you?"

Cutter brushed past his cell mate without answering. He needed space.

With a look of curiosity he didn't bother to hide, the cell-block guard slid the bars shut, turned the key and walked away, eager to tell his buddies that something had finally gotten to Iceman Cutter. Something pretty damn awful, by the looks of the man's white face and wild eyes.

Eldridge leaned against the bars, a worried frown between his black brows. "Talk to me, Cutter. You got the look of a man 'bout to make a powerful mistake."

Cutter prowled the cell, unable to settle. He paused, lit a cigarette, then began pacing again, dragging smoke into his lungs. He'd been smoking too much. His throat was as raw as it had been after three days of fighting the forest fire.

He stubbed out the butt in the can on the table, shoved his hands into his back pockets and confronted Eldridge with a furious scowl. "You got any more of that black lightning you made?"

"Thought you said drinkin' in here made a man careless?"

Cutter trained his gaze on one of the best friends he'd ever had. Under the laser-bright force of Cutter's stare, Clarence Eldridge, two hundred ninety pounds of solid muscle and leashed violence, took an involuntary step backward.

"Something tells me this has to do with your woman," he said.

"She's not my woman."

A child of the ghetto and a veteran of more than one gang war, Clarence had lived to the ripe old age of twenty-six by knowing when to keep his mouth shut. Without another word, he walked to his locker, dug around in the back and pulled out a small sealed plastic bag half-filled with dark liquid, which he handed over in silence.

The bootleg whiskey was made of prunes and potato peelings. It scalded Cutter's throat like acid and burned like fury in his gut. He drank it all, reeling under the quick hit of alcohol. It didn't help.

Like a man just sentenced to hard labor for the rest of his life, he walked frozen-faced and numb to the toilet, dropped the bag into the bowl and flushed it away.

Then, with a strangled cry, he smashed his fist into the cement wall.

Twelve

"I still hate hiking," Regan muttered as she trudged up the porch steps to the new better-than-ever cabin. Tired and hot, she stood for a moment by the railing and lifted her wind-tangled hair away from her neck to let the breeze cool her skin.

It was dusk, and the air was filled with bird song. New grass covered the scorched earth, and the air was sun-washed and sparkling clear.

The cabin's redwood siding carried the rich aroma of freshly milled lumber. The windows had sparkling white caulking. A new state-of-the-art generator hummed merrily away in the shed. Inside, the furniture, the appliances, the things in the cabinets, were sparkling new. Compulsive as always, Philip had thought of everything, right down to the brand new CB radio sitting by the bed.

Dear Philip, she thought with a fond smile. What would she have done without him these past eight months? He'd dried enough tears to fill the Bay, pampered her, bullied her,

invited her to one glitzy bash after another in order to keep
her from brooding.

Life goes on, she thought with a smile that wanted to be
bitter but couldn't quite manage it. Life without Jake Cutter.

Some days had been better than others. In the beginning
they'd been uniformly awful, but as the weeks turned into
months, she'd gradually felt her natural optimism returning.

Following a tip from one of her clients, she'd unearthed
an old Jaguar XK-150 in a farmer's garage in Petaluma. The
lean mean machine had been cannibalized for parts, and
sparrows had made a nest in the upholstery, but it had been
love at first sight.

The fact that she and the farmer had haggled for two
weeks over the price made it all the more special. Restoring
the engine had occupied her mind and tired her body so that
she could stand sleeping alone again. Sanding the Jag's big
fenders and pounding out the dings had helped her forget
the letters that never came and the phone that didn't ring.

Today was September 14. Jake had been out of prison for
two days. San Diego was only a two-hour drive away. If he
were coming, he would have been here by now.

Regan closed her eyes on a rush of sadness. She loved him
so much. She longed to reach out to him, to help him heal.
But the demons inside him had won. In order to survive,
he'd denied his emotions so savagely, so completely, that he
no longer believed in love.

He'd called it stress, gratitude, lust, probably a dozen
other names, just so he could deny it was real. And because
he didn't believe love was real, he couldn't accept her love,
no matter how much she longed to give it to him.

She walked to the railing and ran her hand over the new
wood. Today was a marker for her. The end of her griev-
ing. The day she put Jake Cutter and the pain he'd caused
her out of her heart once and for all.

She'd come here to hold a wake, to bury her memories of their time here, to put an end to her mourning, so that she could get on with the future. By the time she left the mountains, she intended to have all her ghosts safely buried once and for all.

"Right?" she said to a red-tailed hawk watching her from the top of a burned-out pine. As though in answer, the haughty creature spread his wings and turned his head to the sky.

Regan burst out laughing. "Yeah, I know. I affect most untamed creatures like that."

Unable to help herself, she gave another quick look around. The glade was deserted. The new road that had been bulldozed up the mountain was empty.

Oh, Jake! she cried out in her heart. Why couldn't you have fought just a little harder to believe?

She felt the telltale burn of tears behind her eyes. Her vision blurred.

"This has gone on long enough," she muttered as she opened the door and went inside. She hadn't taken more than two steps before she realized something was wrong.

There was a man stretched out on the new brass bed, his big hands propped behind his head, looking for all the world as though he owned the place.

He was dressed in tan jeans and a yellow Oxford-cloth shirt with a button-down collar and rolled-up sleeves. A brand-new pair of shiny cordovan loafers were on the rug by the bed.

This time he was wide awake and watching her with hauntingly familiar hazel eyes.

When she spoke his name with a soft gasp of surprise, Cutter's mouth slanted into a half smile.

"Hello, Regan." His voice was very deep, very soft.

A dozen different emotions raced through her like wildfire. She didn't try to sort through them. They would be there later, waiting for her, after she'd found out why Jake had changed his mind and come to her.

"What are you doing here?"

Her stubborn chin stayed raised, making the sexy little cleft more pronounced. Her green eyes lost the first shimmer of joy, only to turn distant.

Fighting the most important battle of my life, Cutter wanted to say, but the words were stuck someplace behind the lump in his throat. He'd thought about this moment for so long that he was having trouble controlling his emotions.

For the past month he'd lain awake night after night in a cold sweat, trying to figure out how he was going to survive if she'd given up on him. A dozen times he'd begun a letter, only to tear it up. He needed to apologize in person.

He vaulted off the bed, closed the distance between them in three angry strides and stood with feet wide, hands on hips, looking for all the world like a man spoiling for a fight.

"I'm here because, dammit, I can't get you out of my head. I haven't won a chess game since you walked out on me. I haven't slept worth a damn, and I nearly blew my first appointment with my parole officer this morning because I kept thinking about making love to you."

Regan stared at his stiff off-center smile and felt something stirring deep inside her. But the long months of silence had instilled a new caution in her.

"Sounds like you have a problem, Cutter."

So they were back to last names. He felt an icy hand scrape down his back. He was losing her. Correction, he'd blasted her out of his life. For her own good, he'd told himself.

It hadn't taken him long to figure out the real reason. He'd been a damn coward, afraid to take what she'd been offering, afraid to open himself up again.

Damn, did he have to learn everything the hard way? It would serve him right if she sent him packing. It would also kill him.

He reached out to grab a handful of soft caramel curls. Her scent wound around him like the warm silk of her hair, soothing some of the raw places on his soul.

"I made a stupid mistake," he told her bluntly, without excuses. "One I've regretted every day since." Admitting he was wrong had always come hard for him, but he would hire a skywriter to spell it out for the whole world if she would just smile for him.

"I trusted you," she said in a sad voice. "I told you things I'd never told anyone else. I was so sure you wouldn't hurt me."

Her soft voice faded into silence. She looked up at him with all the hurt of eight long months shining in her grass-green eyes.

Cutter clenched his jaw on a wave of anguish worse than anything prison could inflict. "I'll do penance for you if that's what it takes to convince you to give me another chance." His own voice was ragged. "I'll get down on my knees, court you, plead, anything you want. Only stop looking at me like I'm a stranger."

Regan was afraid to trust the naked look of pain that shimmered between his dense blond lashes.

"You *are* a stranger. We knew each other all of three days."

"Three days and three nights. Every night since then I've thought about you and missed you and ached for you until I thought I would explode."

"Then why did you send me away?" she cried, her cheeks heating. "I wanted to be there for you, to help keep you strong the way you kept me strong on the mountain. But you wouldn't let me." Her voice shook. "I think that's what hurt most of all."

His sigh sounded torn from him. "I know that. I saw it in your face when . . . when you looked around that place. I knew you understood how I felt locked up where I couldn't get to the sun or even to fresh air. There were times—" He stopped and drew a ragged breath, showing her without words just how difficult it was to speak of such things. She touched his hand, and his strong fingers closed over hers.

"There were times when I wanted you there so badly I was sick with it. But I'd had so much rage bottled up in me for so long, I was afraid it would explode someday when you were in the way. I couldn't risk that. I had to fight my way through those last months alone."

She wound her arms around his lean waist and buried her face against his shoulder. "I love you, Jake. I never stopped."

Cutter's breath wedged in his throat. His whole body froze in the instant before his breath finally came out in a husky ragged sound.

"Thank God," he whispered before finding her mouth with his. Pleasure radiated through her like the heat of the high desert sun, melting the last of the ice encasing her heart.

He kissed her until they were both breathless. "I can't make it without you, Regan Delaney. I need you."

"I need you, too," she whispered, tracing the familiar line of his mouth.

He played with her hair, running the warm strands through his fingers until they were curling wildly around her face the way they had been that first day, when she'd torn into him for being a jerk.

"What did you call me when we met? An idiot?"

"Mmm. You were, too. I couldn't stand you. I can't imagine what changed my mind."

As soon as he saw her slow soft smile warm into a golden flame in her eyes, he started to breathe again. Even though he'd walked through the prison gates two days ago, he hadn't felt free, really free, until this moment.

"I've been paroled to the Bay Area," he told her quietly. The serenity of the cabin was disorienting him. He had a feeling it would be a long time before he got used to having silence and space around him again.

"To San Francisco?"

"Wherever you live. You're my home now, Regan. I need to be close to you, to be able to touch you when things get bad. To talk to you when I get restless. I have this need to hang on to you right now."

She hid the pain his quiet words struck in her with a pert grin. "Sounds exciting."

His grin flashed. "Later, woman. We've got some serious talking to do."

"Orders, you're always giving me orders." She was so happy she felt giddy. He was really here. He believed!

Jake nuzzled his chin against her forehead. The need in him was prowling hotter, but first he had to get all the hurdles behind him. He wanted to start clean.

"That's why it took me two days to get to you. I had to talk my way into a special consideration. Otherwise, I would have had to serve my parole in San Diego County."

"Was it difficult for you, asking for a favor?"

"Not difficult. Frustrating. I kept worrying that you wouldn't be here."

"I almost wasn't. I wasn't sure I could handle it if...if you didn't come."

A twisting look of regret tore across his face. "I'd give anything if I could take back those words I said to you. Even when I said them, I knew they weren't true."

"So did I. You can't lie worth a darn."

His jaw dropped, and then he laughed. The sound was surprisingly infectious and made his harsh features almost boyish. Something caught in her chest, something hard and hurting. She would make sure he laughed often from now on.

To seal her private vow, Regan framed his face with her hands and arched against him, trying to get closer. His mouth yielded to hers, just as a part of him would always yield to her. Because he loved her.

His body swelled and hardened, but still he made no move to make love to her. When he finally pulled away, her eyes were glittering, and they were both breathing hard. He leaned against the brass footboard and pulled her against him, her legs inside his. Regan shivered at the familiar feel of his long powerful thighs and ready hardness pressed against her so intimately.

Her finger touched the tiny nick by his mouth where he'd cut himself shaving. He smelled of soap, and for once his thick unruly hair looked almost neat. Had he done all that for her? To impress her? To win her back? The lump in her throat thickened.

"I want you, Regan, more than you will ever be able to understand. But you have to know how it is with me."

"Tell me," she whispered, her hands twining around his neck. "I'm listening."

His quick smile was like a gift, one she would always treasure. "It won't be easy. I intend to become a counselor for juvenile offenders someday, but it'll take me years before I get my degree. In the meantime, I have to serve a year on parole, another five on supervised probation. It'll get to me sometimes, having my movements restricted, having to report every week. I can't promise I won't take it out on you. I'll try not to, but—"

Regan pressed her fingers against his mouth. "Let's take it one day at a time. This day I just want to celebrate."

She felt him frown and withdrew her hand. "I'll always be an ex-con, Regan. No matter what I do from here on, there will be times when that will come back to haunt us. I can't pretend it won't hurt, because it will."

"Are you asking me if I can handle your past?"

"Something like that, yes."

She forced herself to meet his shuttered look with her best smile. "I can handle yours if you can handle mine."

His head came up. "Yours? There's nothing to be ashamed of in your past."

"There's nothing in yours, either, Jake. Not one blasted thing. And if I ever hear you even suggest that there is, I'll...I'll put my fist through that stubborn, gorgeous, clean-shaven jaw of yours, you idiot."

An emotion too deep, too savage, for words ripped through him. "Listen, lady. I'm trying to warn you off. You'd be crazy to marry a guy like me."

She held him tighter, loving the clean male scent of him. "There are those who would say the same about you. Tony, for one."

"Tony is a fool!"

"He's also a man, and most men want children."

He took her arms and held her away from him so that she could see his face. Tenderness shone in his eyes, along with another even more powerful emotion. "I have a child, Regan, and I can't wait for the two of you to meet."

"But you said . . . has her mother stopped fighting you?"

He shook his head. "But that won't stop me. If Sinclair won't help, I'll find someone who will. I'm not giving up my daughter."

Regan fought back tears of joy—for Jake, and for his daughter, too. "I'm so glad," she whispered. "And we'll make it work. I know we will. After all, if a twenty-five thousand acre forest fire couldn't stop us, nothing can. Right?"

He smiled at that. His smiles seemed to come easier now. He was the same, and yet he was different. In some indefinable way, he seemed more at peace with himself. The lines in his face were etched deeper, but the driving anger around his mouth was gone.

And most of the shadows had left his eyes, but not all. It would be a long time before they were gone—if ever. But she would work on him, this tender-tough man who loved her, even if he was too scarred, too wary of hurt, to let himself say the words.

He took a deep breath, then said, "I'm going to take the job Sinclair offered me."

She grinned. "Hold out for an outrageous salary. He really needs you."

This time his smile had a rueful slant. "Money's not important to me. It never was. I just need to feel useful, to know that I can make a difference somehow."

She heard the unspoken question and smiled. "Don't worry. I make pots of money selling the cars I restore."

He glanced toward the window. "Whose is that outside?"

"Yours, if you want it. If you don't, we'll sell it."

He traced her smile with his knuckle. "Son of a gun, if I'd known you were rich, as well as sexy and smart and adorable and impossible, I would have let you catch me a lot sooner."

"Catch *you?* Hey, who came after whom here?"

"You invited me."

Her mouth turned stubborn. "You turned me down. Therefore, you came here uninvited. That means you're chasing me."

"So tell me, how am I doing?"

"I'm not sure. Better keep trying." She pretended indecision, but Cutter saw the happiness in her eyes. He tried to smile, but the last months without her had taken the few emotional reserves he'd had left. He felt stripped bare, exposed. He felt a violent need to run for cover, to hide the pain that twisted inside him whenever thoughts of his lost years began closing in on him.

Cutter shut his eyes against a violent surge of emotion. He crushed her to him. "They nearly broke me in that pit. The walls kept closing in. I couldn't breathe. And then you would be there, holding me, smiling down at me. I would feel your hands on my face. I could feel your body next to mine, keeping the blackness from choking me. Sometimes it was hours before I could stop shaking, but as long as you were there with me, in my thoughts, I was all right."

He dragged in a long stream of air, then raised his head and surrendered his gaze to hers.

"I need you to heal me, my sweet, adorable, crazy Regan. I need you to help me forget all the things I had to do in that place to come out alive."

Regan felt tears spill onto her cheeks. "We'll do it together, Jake. We'll start over right now, from this moment, the two of us. We'll make memories together, so beautiful you won't be able to remember anything else."

His face grew still. "This isn't a dream, is it? Because, God help me, I can't stand one more day without you."

"Neither can I."

With a soft murmur, she moved out of his arms. Boldly, confident in his love, she led him to the bed. As he undressed, she reveled in the raw masculine beauty of his wide virile chest, his flat firm belly, his lean hard flanks.

She started to remove her own clothing, but he stopped her. He undressed her with exquisite slowness, his hands and his mouth worshipping each part of her that was bared until she was quivering with need.

"Love me," she murmured against the pulse that throbbed in his throat. "I need you inside me."

He kissed her, then framed her face with his hands. "I love you," he whispered hoarsely. "And I'm never letting you go again."

"I love you, too. So much."

She saw his face change. "I think I'm finally beginning to believe you."

"If you don't, you soon will."

He dragged her against him, his mouth finding hers. By the time he lifted her gently onto the mattress and settled down beside her, her blood was racing, heating her skin. He kissed her over and over, whispering the loving words she'd been so certain he would never say. His touch awakened fires in every hidden, unawakened part of her until she was weak with wanting him.

Later, as they lay entwined, Cutter closed his eyes and listened to Regan's even, peaceful breathing. She was asleep, her head pillowed on his chest, her hand nestled trustingly in his.

Slowly he let his gaze rove to the window. A gentle drizzle beat against the panes. The air smelled clean.

His arms tightened protectively around Regan's soft, warm body. She stirred, smiling in her sleep.

Jake kissed her gently. So this is love, he thought, and smiled. In every way that mattered, she was already his wife. But as soon as he could get her to a church, she would have his ring on her finger. And then, he would spend the rest of his life making sure she always felt loved and cherished. The same way she made him feel at this moment.

Jake closed his eyes and settled Regan more firmly against him. Four years, he thought. He'd survived. No, he'd done better than that. He'd found Regan.

The empty years stretching out behind him began to fade. The cold hazel eyes that had been haunted too long by terrible twisted visions began to warm. The hard unyielding mouth that had forgotten how to smile softened.

The man who had cared too much, the man who had suffered unbearable agony alone and in silence for so long, began to heal.

*   *   *   *   *

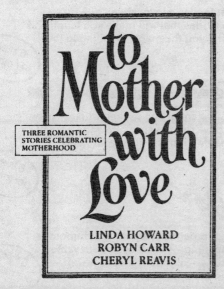

FOUR UNIQUE SERIES
FOR EVERY WOMAN YOU ARE...

Silhouette Romance®

Love, at its most tender, provocative,
emotional... in stories that will make you laugh and
cry while bringing you the magic of falling in love.

6 titles per month

Silhouette Special Edition®

Sophisticated, substantial and packed with
emotion, these powerful novels of life and love will
capture your imagination and steal your heart.

6 titles per month

SILHOUETTE *Desire*®

Open the door to romance and passion. Humorous,
emotional, compelling—yet always a believable
and sensuous story—Silhouette Desire never
fails to deliver on the promise of love.

6 titles per month

SILHOUETTE·INTIMATE·MOMENTS®

Enter a world of excitement, of romance
heightened by suspense, adventure and the
passions every woman dreams of. Let us
sweep you away.

4 titles per month

Take 4 bestselling love stories FREE

Plus get a FREE surprise gift!

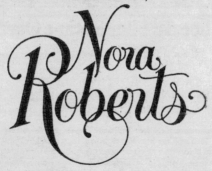
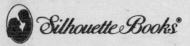